2025

"City of Gold"

S. D. Burke

Thanks for taking the adventure!
Sylvia Burke

2025 City of Gold
by S.D. Burke

Printed in the United States of America

ISBN 9781619969421

Unless otherwise indicated, Bible quotations are taken from the New American Standard Version of the Bible. Copyright © 1960, 1962, 1963, 1968, 1971, 1972, 1973 by The Lockman Foundation, LaHabra, Calif.

www.xulonpress.com

I would like to dedicate 2025 City of Gold to my grand-children—Matthew, Lindsay, Natalie, Eric Daniel, Madelynne, Aubrey, Hannah, Tori, Ryan and Collin. May the Lord keep you as the apple of His eye and may you dwell under the shadow of the Almighty's wings.

Acknowledgments

Aspecial thanks...
to all who read *2025 The Guardian* and asked me "when will Book II be out." You kept me on track.

to our daughter Jodie, a professional writer in Hollywood, who set the standard high for *City of Gold* and was my inspiration and story editor. I appreciate all her patience and wisdom.

to Xulon Press for putting out a beautiful book.

To Donna Goodrich, who made room in her busy schedule to line edit City of Gold so that it could be published this Spring.

to my children who act as missionaries in their cities to bring the message of this trilogy to the world.

And to my dear husband who encourages me, is patient with my time at the computer, and who fields not only grammar and spelling questions but who gives me good critique as needed.

Prologue

Daniel Jordan stared at the vacant eyes looking back at him in the mirror. He set his razor down on the bathroom counter and absently rubbed his clean jaw. Was it Thursday or Friday? Out of habit, he reached for his medicine noticing Dr. Chang's name on the label. Dr. Chang, the psychiatrist who'd overseen Daniel's treatment at the Fort Thompson retraining center—his powerful enemy.

He shook out his usual dose and stared at the pills in the palm of his hand. Tears of anger stung his eyes. He'd betrayed himself. As a high school Olympic athlete Daniel signed a pledge never to take drugs. If any athlete failed a blood test, he was immediately expelled from the team. From the first dose, even though he was no longer a competitive soccer player, Daniel felt like a criminal compromising everything he held sacred.

Warned to follow the treatment program by Ben, his Guardian trainer, Daniel cooperated. Ben had watched others resist and it only made the doctors increase the strength of the drugs and lengthen the treatments. Daniel remembered Ben's words, "You've got no control here. They own you. Go with the program, so you can get out in one piece." It was the only reason Daniel had taken the drugs. The side effects made him feel like a zombie, a dead man walking. The drugs altered his thinking, making him struggle for thoughts.

Well, today he could resist. *This is for you, Coach,* Daniel thought as he emptied the vial into the john. Flushing the meds down the toilet was a step at regaining control over his body. Daniel started to put on the orange scrubs that he'd lived in for the last six months but caught himself. *Would he ever be able to think clearly again? Get a grip, Daniel,* he thought. *It's over.*

He looked around and saw his Guardian uniform pressed and laying on the bed. Someone must have brought it in when he was in the shower. He walked slowly over to the uniform, wishing with all his heart that it was a pair of jeans and a sweatshirt and that he was going home to help his dad with the ranch.

Beside the uniform sat a small white box. Daniel took off the lid and discovered the watch his dad had given him for graduation. He turned the watch over and read his father's words, "Be true to yourself." He snapped on the watch... time to start living that mantra.

The box also contained the arrowhead Grandpa gave him at the Ascension that he'd carried in the pocket of his uniform for luck. Rubbing it between his fingers, he slipped it into his pocket. Fresh memories of Grandpa washed over his mind, memories the administration tried to erase with medication and brain treatments, but Daniel would never forget Grandpa and Gram.

Who in Daniel's high school graduating class would have thought Daniel would end up a prisoner in a military mental hospital? He was the guy voted Most Likely To Succeed, the guy scouted by three professional soccer teams, the guy who planned to see the world.

Anger gave Daniel the strength to hold on each day. He'd lied to the doctors pretending he'd forgotten the Ascension, hoping they wouldn't crank up the intensity of the laser treatments.

"Dressed yet, Daniel?"

"No sir, not yet."

"You don't have to call me sir, Daniel. I'm a Guardian just like you. Today's your big day, buddy."

Daniel's blank look shocked Ben. "I told you that you'd make it." Ben patted him on the shoulder. "You made it, man."

The Guardian uniform hung on Daniel. He weighed 185 when he came to the hospital but he doubted that he weighed 140 now. "Captain Taylor said I'm taking a new duty at the capital, some kind of Youth Council."

Ben looked puzzled. *Wasn't Daniel being sent home to recuperate?* "In the City of Gold?"

"No, in the capital."

"But Daniel, the capital is the City of Gold. If they are sending you there, it's a chance of a lifetime. Only a few people have seen it. It's been designed by the president himself. Rumor has it, it's really sci-fi. I can't believe they are sending you there. Maybe I should switch places with you. I'd give anything to get out of here. How did you get that assignment?"

In truth Daniel didn't know. All he knew was that Captain Taylor offered two options for Guardian duty: Stay at the retraining center and work as a Guardian, or go back to Luke and help train new cadets. He'd told Daniel that under no circumstances could he send Daniel back to the Center for New Age Medicine because of the Guardian's work on the Ascensions.

Daniel asked not to stay at the retraining center, and possibly there was no opening at the school for Guardians. Then at one of his meetings, Captain Taylor informed Daniel that he'd sent his academic record from high school, his athletic participation in the High School Olympics, and the recommendations from his principal, coaches, and teachers to be considered as Arizona's senator to the Youth Council, an assignment the Captain felt matched Daniel's personality better. These were the same records that initially got Daniel appointed as the Arizona Guardian, but the Captain sent nothing of his six months at the Fort Thompson Retraining Center. The competition would be tough but there was a chance. To Daniel's total amazement, he was selected for the Youth Council to represent Arizona.

A small stabbing pain in Daniel's head brought him back to reality reminding him of the excruciating pain the LBTs caused and the hours he'd lost from having his brain fried. It was a miracle he was still alive, much less healthy enough to be officially released. "Guess I'm ready."

Ben touched the keypad on the wall with a special code that changed every day. The metal door to Daniel's room slid open and they stepped into the hall. Still feeling the effects of the drugs and treatment, Daniel stumbled down the hall behind his Guardian friend.

When they reached the helicopter, Daniel turned to shake hands with Ben. But Ben put his arms around his friend and gave him a big hug. "Good luck Daniel. No more trouble, huh?"

Chapter One

T he glaring sun blinded Daniel as he waited on the tarmac for the pilot. He took a last look around his beloved Arizona desert, wishing he could go home for a month and get over the effects of the treatments. Trained as a soldier, Daniel drew strength that this ordeal — like any other assignment — was finished. He was still a Guardian until he reached the capital. But he was confused. *What did Ben mean that he was going to the City of Gold? What happened to Washington D.C.? What kind of a name was City of Gold for the capital of the United States?* Lost in his thoughts, he was interrupted by a voice.

"Hey, buddy, you my passenger to the capital?"

Daniel gazed into the weary eyes of a sixty-some-year-old man dressed in faded jeans and a Harley Davidson

T-shirt, surprised the pilot wasn't military and that his transport to the City of Gold was in a vintage Boeing chopper.

"Yeah…I guess I am, Daniel Jordan."

Seeing the kid look him over, the pilot said, "Expecting a military escort? Well, this is your lucky day; you get to ride in Old Glory."

"What kind of plane is this?" Daniel asked.

"Not a plane, son, a cargo helicopter. She's carried marines and supplies all over the world, even in Iraq. Old Glo's a faithful bird, a Boeing CH 46 Sea Knight, 1960 vintage, to be exact."

Daniel smiled as Jerry patted the belly of the old helicopter, finished his last minute checks, and turned to Daniel.

"Shove your backpack in between those exotics and climb in." Daniel slid in between a prickly pear cactus and a bird-of-paradise climbing into the co-pilot's seat. The entire plane was filled with southwestern desert plants.

"What's with the plants?" Daniel asked.

"The administration is getting ready for some big TV presentation in the capital. These boys are the finishing touch. The one good thing is—they give off oxygen, lots of oxygen."

Jerry watched Daniel sink into his seat and try to buckle his seat belt. The young Guardian's hands shook with the effort.

"You all right, kid? You aren't going to heave on me, are you?"

Daniel stopped, too weak to slide the seat belt together. "No...I don't think so."

Jerry leaned over, grasped the seat belt and shoved it together until it clicked. He felt sorry for the kid and wondered what the wackos had done to him in the funny farm. He pushed the engine starter button and the helicopter blades began to whirr.

"So...you ready for the big adventure?" Jerry yelled.

"Yeah, I can stand the change."

Jerry frowned. *Should he warn this kid that all would not be roses in the new capital? Or that he wouldn't be the pilot for the administration, if the Prophet hadn't blackmailed him into service by agreeing to keep his mother off the Ascension rolls.*

Daniel noticed the scowl on Jerry's face. "Do you live in Phoenix, Jerry?"

"Ever since my mom bought a place in Sun City."

So Jerry's mom was old and lived in Sun City. Daniel thought of his grandparents. "Is she well?"

Jerry gave him a look. "No, kid, she's wearing out, you know. Her body could stand some new parts but..."

Daniel looked away. "My grandparents were in the 1st Ascension. They wouldn't give my grandma a heart operation when she had a stroke."

Jerry nodded. That was the way it worked for old people now.

"Been to the biosphere?" he asked Daniel.

"No, just read about it. It was an experiment under a dome. Kind of like a green prison for the scientists that got assigned there."

"You got it. The new capital is kinda like that. Don't say I told you, but this here City of Gold is a prison too. Can't get in or out without high security."

"Really?" Daniel wondered why an entire city would be under lockdown. How could it even be possible?

"You read the Bible?" Jerry looked over at Daniel. "Oh, course not. You were one of the Bible burners, weren't you? Well, the City of Gold looks like paradise, but it's a fraud. 'City of Darkness' I call it, spewing out evil for the whole world. Bunch of elitists planning the future of us normals. Taking away our rights to health and happiness."

They fell into an uneasy silence. Exhausted, Daniel's head fell forward and he drifted off into a deep sleep. For two hours he slept until a sudden jerk jarred him awake.

Jerry cursed sharply under his breath. "A whiteout. A wall of snow," he mumbled.

The helicopter was caught in a blizzard. Suddenly, out of the fog, Daniel saw an iridescent dome open before them. Strong magnets drew the helicopter onto a landing pad on the roof of one of the buildings.

"Go ahead, Daniel," the pilot instructed, "this is where you get out. Someone will be along shortly to take you where you're going."

Daniel jumped down from the cockpit of the helicopter and stood transfixed by the golden city sprawled below him.

Seeing Daniel's amazement, Jerry asked, "Didn't anyone tell you the president and his crew moved the capital inland? What you are looking at is the new capital of the US of A — the City of Gold, located right here in the breadbasket of the country, good old Kansas."

Jerry got to work unloading the exotic plants. Daniel watched the older man work for a moment, then started to help him. "No, kid, I got it covered. That's why they pay me the big bucks. Save your energy. Your escort should be here in a few minutes."

Daniel stood gaping at the modern metropolis before him. The whole capital was enclosed under a giant overhead dome. Light refracted off the blue glass buildings, creating rainbows everywhere he looked. Each building had a unique design; some had rooftop gardens and pools; others, massive stain-glassed windows. In the middle of the city, Daniel saw a golden statue but from his distant viewpoint on the landing pad of the multistory building they'd landed on, he couldn't identify who it resembled. The giant dome provided a natural greenhouse even in winter for plants that never took root in Kansas before: palm trees, bougainvillea, bird-of-paradise, orchids, and lilies.

Instead of traditional cars, strange metallic vehicles glided soundlessly along the streets pulled by solar rays ricocheting off the forty-foot golden sculpture. A stream wound its way under footbridges and streets appeared to be glass block with threads of gold.

Seeing Daniel's astonishment, Jerry stopped unloading the plants and asked, "So what do you think?"

Daniel whistled low under his breath. "This has to be the most futuristic city you could ever dream of...like someone tried to design their idea of heaven."

In the distance, but still under the dome, Daniel saw vineyards, orchards, wheat fields, and herds of cattle. The capital appeared self-sustaining. From his military training, Daniel realized a capital located inland would be easier to protect from nuclear missiles. This beautiful city, so different from Washington, D.C., shocked him more than the laser brain treatments ever had. He leaned over the edge of the roof to get a better view of the golden statue, when a tap on the shoulder caused him to lose his balance. A strong hand grabbed his uniform and pulled him away from the railing. He turned to find an auburn-haired Guardian with giant freckles spreading across his face.

"Alex Gordon, here to save your life," he said.

Daniel regained his balance and grinned. "Good reflexes, Alex. Thanks."

"No problem. It's a little too soon to jump, isn't it?"

The pilot walked over to Alex. "Well, I see you got your recruit."

"He's not my recruit, Jerry. Daniel's the new Youth Council senator from Arizona."

The pilot's face clouded. "Thought you were one of us, son. Didn't realize you were one of them. Well, think I'll get myself a brew. And…forget the junk I told you, just running off at the mouth. Sure you'll fit right in this paradise." Shoulders slumped, Jerry walked off.

"Don't mind him. He's running out of gas. Hates these prickly pear flights, if you know what I mean. Welcome to the City of Gold. It's pretty incredible, isn't it?"

"It's the coolest place I've ever seen. I didn't know we had a new capital or that the Guardians had duty here."

Alex stared at him. "Where you been, man. Ever since terrorists bombed the Statue of Liberty…"

Daniel blanked out. *What else had happened while he was in Fort Thompson?*

Alex patted him on the shoulder. "It's perfect here, Daniel. You'll love it."

Jerry had to be wrong. Daniel's hopes rose. Maybe his mother was right. This president was creative. He was taking America into a new era. The pain of his early Guardian years and the deaths of his grandparents were in the past. A great weight lifted off Daniel. He remembered Captain Taylor's words as he left Fort Thompson, "It's up to you now, Daniel."

"I'll do my best, Captain. Thanks for giving me another chance."

Chapter Two

D aniel and Alex headed for the glass elevator off the helipad. Daniel hoped Alex wouldn't ask too many questions about his experience in the Guardians.

"How'd you get assigned to the Youth Council?" Alex asked.

"Beats me...long story. This where I live?" The two stopped in front of one of the one-story units whose tall solar roofs opened and closed automatically. Blown away by the design Daniel asked, "What makes them open and close?"

"Computer controls everything—humidity, temperature." Alex pulled out a passkey and handed it to Daniel. "This will get you into any place in the city. It has your thumbprint and iris scan. Won't get you into other people's rooms, just yours, and normal places like the dining room, auditorium, and the gym."

"Alex, anyplace off limits? I can walk around and not get into trouble?"

"You just entered paradise, man. We got no trouble here. Almost anything goes. I'll show you around your suite and then maybe we can go somewhere for a drink. You twenty-one?"

"No, not yet."

They entered the apartment. On one wall, a virtual fireplace burned, flames flickering in welcome. A glass wall looked out on a gently moving waterway. Daniel opened the door to listen as the water cascaded over a waterfall surrounded by rose-colored flowering bushes. Alex showed him how to camouflage the window wall for privacy.

A small kitchenette contained a loaded food butler. "Just like home," Alex laughed.

Daniel studied the controls on the wall.

"Sound system and mood enhancer," explained Alex.

"Mood enhancer?"

"Yeah, feel like blue skies, green woods, snow on the mountains, push this control and the walls will reflect your mood. I'm tellin' you, paradise, man. Ready to check out the city? I'll take you to my favorite place."

They strolled around the city, walking over footbridges that straddled the flowing waterways until they came to an outdoor café. Taking a seat, Alex ordered a malted beer while Daniel ordered a smoothie. A Latin trio played sensual calypso music. The boys relaxed, enjoying their drinks.

For the first time, Daniel realized there were girls in the City of Gold. "Do they work here?" Daniel asked.

"Some do, some are Youth Council like you."

The boys leaned back and studied a group of girls gyrating to the pulsing bongo drums. Alex watched Daniel. "How long has it been?"

Daniel's face turned red. "A long time." Then he saw her, a girl with dark shoulder-length hair wearing an off-the-shoulder sundress with big blue flowers splashed over it. She turned and for a moment their eyes connected. A girl who looked exactly like Ariel, the clairvoyant sent by the administration of Fort Thompson to assess Daniel's mental state. She nodded at Daniel, sending shivers down his spine. *Was she a plant sent from the administration?* Suspicion seeped into his bloodstream.

Alex called him back to the present. "Check the number on your passkey, Daniel. When the waiter comes, write down that number. Same thing whenever you have a meal. No cash needed here. Did you get your number?"

"No, will I need it?"

Alex studied Daniel. "Everyone here has a number. You'll have till you're twenty-one to get it. Security…no dissidents allowed."

Weary from the long day, Daniel got up, thanked Alex for the tour, and returned to his apartment, glad to be alone. The brain treatments left him unable to hold a conversation for a long time. He collapsed in the comfortable leather lounge chair next to the fireplace. The flames looked real, reminding Daniel of the ranch and his family in Phoenix.

Barely able to keep his eyes open, he programmed the kitchen butler. A giant hamburger deluxe fell out of the chute. He added some French fries and settled down to watch the evening news. All the major networks appeared to be broadcasting as Global News Network. *Did that mean the president was controlling the media? Or just the news? What happened to Fox and the other networks?*

A debate in the U.N. caught his attention. Evidently, world leaders were discontent to have the U.N. in the United

States. As he listened, the majority of the nations lined up against the U.S. and Israel. The Turkish ambassador spoke out, "Bring the U.N. to the Arab community. We are the peoples of peace. And it will send a signal to the aggressors and our Israeli friends that the Arab world is peace-loving."

The network switched to Iran, Syria and Egypt whose Muslim rulers endorsed the move. *Where was the United States ambassador? Did America support this?* A loud gavel pounded for quiet as the members readied for the vote.

Daniel finished his sandwich. Excited but exhausted, he opened the sliding door on his window wall. Laughter and voices drifted across the stream. *When was the last time he'd been with normal kids having fun?* He let go of the hurt he felt towards his mother for getting him imprisoned at Fort Thompson. Although his appointment to the Youth Council came in a roundabout way, his mother's hopes and dreams for him were coming true.

Still dressed in his Guardian uniform, Daniel fell onto the bed while the TV droned on, the flames of the virtual fireplace casting shadows on the wall.

President Blackstone turned the satellite program off. Fools, they were playing right into his hands. He'd instructed his U.N. ambassador to vote with the majority. The U.N. would be moved to Bagdad, a sign of recognition to the quasi-freedom America fought for in the Iraq war.

Now all despots removed, the Muslim world would be looking for a leader, a world leader. And this was the headquarters from which the one world government should emerge.

Chapter Three

A sultry mechanical voice awoke Daniel. "My name is Wanda. I'll be your personal alarm. Today you are expected at breakfast at eight a.m. in the rotunda. You will find appropriate clothes in your walk-in closet. Notice the personalized initials. The standard Youth Council wardrobe is slacks, golf shirt, and jacket. Have a nice day."

Well, at least Wanda didn't wake him with mantras. Maybe that would come later, but Daniel hoped not. His head ached as if he had a hangover. Getting off the drugs cold turkey left him confused. Often, he felt like he stood outside the world watching but not part of the action. Noise agitated him and his brain felt like it was flying apart.

Perhaps a shower would help. He shed his wrinkled Guardian uniform and entered the S-shaped shower. In the first part of the shower, Alex said he would find a water massage table to loosen and relax his muscles. In ten minutes, Daniel's body felt great, but his head still throbbed and his hands were shaking. Withdrawal. He recognized the symptoms, seeing it often enough at the Fort. Nauseous and dizzy, his resolve held firm. No drugs. He stepped into the second part of the shower. Water cascaded on his body sounding like the waterfall outside his room. The sound soothed him. His soul longed to be pampered and it looked like that was going to happen here in the City of Gold. He was in a safe place. Jerry was wrong. He *could* have a life here. He put on the khaki pants and a white golf shirt. Despite his weight loss, the clothes fit perfectly. The navy jacket bore the insignia YCA — Youth Council of America. The inside label said Daniel Jordan.

As he left his suite — after checking to see if he had his passkey — he walked slowly in the direction everyone was going. Despite his wish to be normal, Daniel remained tense and suspicious unready to trust anyone and afraid of meeting a Rick or an Ariel.

The glass escalator carried him to the rotunda — a round, glassed-in dining room providing a 360-degree view of the entire city. Daniel wished Alex had warned him that the rotunda restaurant rotated. He stopped to get his balance grabbing a stair rail to steady himself. *How many more side effects would he experience trying to get off this medicine?* Gradually, he regained his balance and joined the line for the breakfast buffet. The aroma of bacon and coffee...he could smell again! And...his appetite was back. At least something good was happening to his body. He loaded up on eggs Benedict, sausage, waffles, fruit, and orange juice, and then felt ashamed. He was starving. Sitting down at a table for two, he listened to the chatter while he ate. He wasn't a loner, but until he got control of his body, he felt safer alone. He ate slowly enjoying every new taste, especially the cinnamon toast, strawberries, and pineapples. Finished, he left the table thankful the food eased the ache in his head.

In the courtyard, a girl with a lapel pin that said "Violet" signaled Daniel to join her group for a tour. As they moved into the Amphitheater, Daniel saw etched in the glass ceiling, a panorama of winged mythological figures armed with fiery swords doing battle. Light illumined the colored glass etchings creating a three-dimensional sculptured painting.

"The action murals on the walls provide a 3D sample of the movie, music group or play that is scheduled," Violet explained. The group stopped in front of a recent release,

"Against the Night," an action thriller with Heidi Murango and Jason Ellis, two popular Hollywood stars. "They take very good care of us here, even bringing us the top Broadway shows and concerts."

Daniel studied the interactive murals, stopping in front of his favorite rock group, *Destiny's Angels*. At least that group appeared as he remembered them. His spirits lifted as he followed Violet into the recreation center. Odd, but seeing the tennis and racketball courts, work-out machines, running track, and lap pool acted like medicine for Daniel. Here was the normal he needed so much. He could get strong and fight the drug reaction the one way he'd always depended on. If he could get the athlete in him healthy, Daniel knew he'd be all right.

The group passed an area for massage therapy. "If any of you guys need touch therapy," Violet said, "we got the best masseurs in the world but you'll have to beat out the old guys. The governors think it's just for them. Schedule a treatment and check it out."

"What about the Q cars," someone asked.

"Sorry, they're just for the governors."

"Finally, this building is where you'll work." Violet led them into the Youth Council chambers. "Each of you is assigned a desk. I think they did it by states." The members' desks formed a semicircle in front of an elongated table with five microphones. Daniel made his way to the front row realizing he'd be in the third seat next to Alabama and Alaska. He was seated directly in front of the table with the mikes on it. A touchpad with keyboard connected each Youth Council member with the huge media wall behind the Prophet.

"Behind this table—which will at some point seat your officers as well as the Prophet—you can see a state-of-the-art communication center for live television or conferences. Your touchpad allows you to use this system as a computer." Violet switched on the system and the room filled with live satellite broadcasting from the Global News Network. "This is an inner city hookup so the president can participate, if he wishes, even from his office. It is also set up for global communication should that be necessary. Any questions? If not, the afternoon is yours. Check the workstation in your condo and you'll find two activities selected for you."

Anxious to see what activities he'd drawn, Daniel brought up the secure website for the City of Gold and entered 1727—the code number that appeared on his passkey. The itinerary showed that he'd drawn racketball and swimming for today's activities. Pleased, Daniel changed into athletic gear and headed for the racket ball courts. He signed in, and was handed a card with Room 7, a racket, and some balls. Surprised to find the beautiful brunette he'd seen dancing at the outdoor café, hair in a ponytail, banging balls into the walls, he hesitated before going into the court.

"Ready for a game," she called.

"Always ready. Daniel Jordan, Phoenix."

"Lydia Cohen. Let's see what you've got."

Daniel and Lydia shook hands and began playing. Lydia showed him no mercy. Daniel quickly gave up the idea of slowing his game and responded to this competitive, athletic girl. He won by a hair but was exhausted.

"Good game," Daniel said, awed that Lydia had almost beaten him. "Where did you learn to play like that?"

"This was my dad's favorite way to spend time with me. He showed me no mercy and...I love the game."

Sweat streaming into their eyes, the two toweled off. "I'm impressed, Miss Cohen."

"What's your next activity?" Lydia asked.

"Swimming laps. Yours?"

"Free time by the pool. Love to swim, but somehow reading a book by the pool sounds good after that workout."

A little uneasy, Daniel grew quiet, unused to competing in sports with girls.

"Did I scare you...the way I played?"

"To be honest, you really surprised me."

"Would that be a chauvinistic reply?" Lydia bantered.

Daniel blushed. *Why did he think girls were only cheerleaders for the guys?* Feeling foolish, he withdrew. She was right. His comment was a little chauvinistic. In truth, he never expected a girl to give him such a game.

"Let's do it again sometime," Lydia called as she turned to walk away. Daniel watched her depart, surprised to see her put her passkey into the lock of a suite a few units down from his. Adrenaline still running high, he dressed in his swim trunks, then grabbed a large bottle of water. At the pool, he laid his towel and water bottle on a chair and dove in. The cool water wrapped around him, taking him into the familiar world most relaxing to him. Losing track of time, he swam until he felt stress-free. When he stepped out, he heard a voice say,

"You're quite a swimmer."

Shaking the water out of his eyes, he looked up to find Lydia reclining in the chair next to his. He ignored her, pretending he hadn't heard.

"Are you always this friendly, Daniel?"

Daniel made the mistake of looking into the clear blue eyes. *Was this girl a spy sent to check him out?* He'd earned the right to be paranoid but the young woman continued. "Remember me? I'm the girl who almost beat you in racketball."

"And you are a Youth Council member?" Daniel asked.

"I am the Youth Council member from San Diego who's going to allow you to take her to dinner tonight."

Not feeling social yet because of his addictions, Daniel shook his head. "Sorry, Lydia, I need to get organized…just going to mellow out tonight."

He watched the friendliness leave her face and the storm clouds move in. *What was he doing?* A beautiful young woman asks him to have dinner with her and he says no? He must really be losing his mind. He started to tell her another time, but hurt, she'd moved on to a group of kids drinking beer and having a good time.

Daniel curled up alone watching a movie while nursing a headache that threatened to explode his head, thanks to the withdrawal from the drugs. He knew Lydia couldn't understand his refusal to take her to dinner. However, it hadn't taken her long to move on and find a group looking for a party.

Loud voices returning from dinner broke through his thoughts. He opened the door of his suite to find Lydia pinned to her door by a muscular jock who wasn't taking no for an answer. Lydia looked frightened as the drunken guy grabbed her by the hair and pulled her to him. He heard her yell "Stop!" and that was all it took.

Daniel yelled at the drunk. "Hey, leave her alone."

The drunken YC member ignored him.

Daniel grabbed him by the shoulders and pulled him off Lydia who quickly took out her passkey and slipped into her apartment.

"What's it your business?" the guy said. "She's fair game."

"She's not a game," Daniel said as he shoved the guy against Lydia's door. "Leave her alone." Not wanting to make an enemy so soon, Daniel took it down a notch. "Hey, buddy, you're drunk. We don't treat women like that. Go back to your suite. Take a cold shower."

Angry now, the guy lunged for Daniel. Daniel's Shotokan attack training automatically kicked in and he swept the guy's legs out from under him in one well-placed kick. Turning, he strode back to his suite. So much for not making an enemy.

Lydia listened through the door still shaking. So...Daniel was a good guy after all.

She didn't go back outside but tomorrow, she'd thank him. How could she know who would turn into a jerk and who was a gentleman? The guy seemed funny and fun. Nevertheless, she'd be more careful in the future.

The next morning, Lydia waited for Daniel to come out of his suite.

"Daniel...I just wanted to thank you for rescuing me."

"Yeah, hope I didn't hurt the guy. Afraid my Guardian training swept him off his feet."

"I didn't know you were a Guardian."

"Yes, I guess the authorities thought I was better material for the Youth Council."

Lydia kicked a stone. "Daniel, can we start over? Would you join me for dinner in the rotunda tonight before Youth Council?"

Realizing Lydia felt embarrassed that he'd had to rescue her, Daniel decided to accept her offer.

"I was planning to dress up for our first Youth Council meeting."

"I'd be honored to take you to dinner, Lydia. I'll pick you up about five-thirty p.m.. That should give us time for dinner before the Youth Council."

Rose linen tablecloths decked the tables of the dining hall. Candlelight flickered on each table creating a formal and romantic atmosphere. Daniel flashed back to the lonely cardboard tasting meals he'd eaten in his windowless, gray prison room. He began to sweat.

"Is everything all right, Daniel?" Lydia said.

"Yeah, sure." He had to stop flashing back. "Just a headache." He held the chair while Lydia sat down. Daniel looked at the beautiful young woman dressed in a one shoulder, white dinner dress, sitting opposite him, convinced that if the administration sent her, he was a dead man.

The menu for the day consisted of two entrees. Daniel chose a New York strip steak while Lydia selected grilled salmon.

"Can you smell the gardenias?" Lydia said. "My mother grows them in her garden. It's her favorite flower."

They ordered and it dawned on Daniel that this was his first date in a year. Lydia put him at ease. He relaxed. She wasn't a spy; she was just a Council member like him.

"How did you become the Youth Council member from California?" Daniel asked.

"Probably same as you, scholar, president of my senior class, organized a few programs for the Boys and Girls Clubs...that sort of thing. I'm sure it didn't hurt that my parents are both renowned research professors. How about you?"

"I really don't know. I was Arizona's representative to the Guardians but I guess the authorities thought I would be better used on the Youth Council so they sent my resume from high school and the Guardians. I was a good student but my only big achievement was playing soccer for the high school Olympics. I worked with my parents to host inner-city kids for camps on our ranch. My parents received a big community award and a lot of notoriety for the camps. I'm sure that didn't hurt either."

After dinner they sauntered to the Youth Council chambers. Donning the sapphire robes handed them, they sat down amid the other Council members. All waited for their first glimpse of Omega I, the president and their benefactor. They didn't have long to wait. They would soon learn Omega I was always punctual. The president wore a dark navy suit, white shirt, and electric blue tie. Strikingly handsome with a small salt-and-pepper beard, he radiated power. Before beginning his address, he surveyed the young Council members.

"You sit before me representing the best America has to offer. I chose each of you to represent our fifty states. You are the strength and hope of America. You will be given much and much will be expected of you. The City of Gold is your home now. It's a way of life designed just for you—total freedom. Your comfort and peace of mind are our objective. Welcome to the City of Gold."

Lydia and Daniel left the Youth Council. For the first time in a long time, Daniel felt at ease. "Feel like a walk?" he asked.

Silhouetted against the night sky, the palm trees formed a tunnel over their heads as they walked. Daniel hadn't trusted anyone for so long he felt wary of speaking his thoughts.

Unlike Daniel, Lydia was transparent and uninhibited. "Daniel?"

"Yes."

"What did you think of Omega I's welcoming speech?"

"The president was impressive. He was trying to make us feel special...chosen. It is an incredible city with everything we could ever dream of or want. They want us to think of it as our new home."

"Yes, but this isn't really our home. I love my parents. To me the City of Gold is kind of a job...but not my home." Lydia frowned. "I don't like it that we can't communicate with our families."

What should Daniel say? He knew the strategy...wean them away from their families...surround them with everything they could ever desire and create a new loyalty to the City of Gold. "They want to be our new family. It was the same in the Guardians. We weren't allowed to talk to family or friends for six months."

The two continued to walk, sitting down on a rustic glider next to the stream. The moonlight sparkled like diamonds on the water. Rocks lining the streambed glowed with a golden light. "What do you think of our City of Gold?"

"It doesn't seem real to me somehow," Lydia said.

"No, it's like we woke up and someone placed us in Oz."

"Oz was in Kansas too, wasn't it?" Lydia giggled. "Have you seen the Wizard of Oz?"

"Oh yes, my grandparents had a wonderful collection of old videos."

"Did you live close to your grandparents?"

"Most of my life they lived in Michigan...they spent the summer before they died with us in Phoenix."

"How sad. Were they in an accident?"

"No, the 1st Ascension. The Center for New Age Medicine received Grandma's records from the hospital when she was admitted for a heart attack. She was too old for surgery."

"But you said both. Your grandpa, too?"

Uncomfortable, Daniel looked away. "Grandpa turned eighty about the same time and volunteered to accompany Grandma Jenny when she was assigned to the Ascension. Grandpa's last act was taking care of Grandma through the Ascension."

Sensing Daniel didn't want to talk about the Ascension, Lydia changed the subject.

"The golden statue of the president is mysterious. What do you think its purpose is?"

"I don't know, but the solar rays from its head power the Q cars. I can only imagine what other technology it's equipped with."

"I think it talks," said Lydia. "I passed it on my way to breakfast and I could swear it spoke to me."

Daniel frowned. He suspected the statue held the key to many secrets of the City of Gold. No doubt the statue was imbedded with cutting-edge technology. He put the statue on a list of things to investigate.

They stopped at Lydia's door. "I had a good time, tonight, Daniel. I hope we can be friends. See you tomorrow."

Daniel kissed Lydia lightly on the cheek. He walked slowly to his apartment. He hadn't slept well since the night the MPs dragged him from the ranch. Perhaps in this new place, with new friends, the nightmare would go away.

Chapter Four

During the night, the world outside the city received a heavy snowfall. Lydia, who had never seen a new snow before, woke up to a blanket of white covering the distant trees. Fascinated with the magical scene, she finished her shower and dressed.

Daniel picked her up for breakfast. As they were leaving the rotunda, Lydia turned to him. "Do you think we could walk outdoors? It's so beautiful. Look at how the trees sparkle in the distance. We don't have snow in San Diego. I'd just like to touch it."

Not sure what the administration allowed, Daniel hesitated. "We could ask for a special pass. See what they say."

The pair inquired at the gate. Frowning, the Guardian on duty looked at them suspiciously.

"Why do you want to leave?"

"We just want to hike in the snow," said Daniel.

"I've never seen a new snowfall," added Lydia.

The Guardian shook his head, not understanding why anyone in their right mind wanted to go into the cold when the temperature in the City of Gold was 75 degrees all the time.

"If you want an adventure, or some alone time, why don't you two sign up for a couples massage."

Lydia looked at Daniel; the guard just didn't get it.

"Look," Lydia explained calmly. "We love our life here in the City of Gold. I just never saw a snow like this, is that so hard to understand?"

At that point, Daniel's friend Alex checked in for duty. "Hey guys, what's up?"

Downcast, Lydia clammed up.

"Alex, meet Lydia. I just wanted to show her a real snow-fall. Take a hike. It's not a plot to escape."

Alex turned to the other guard. "C'mon, Lou, write them a couple of passes." Seeing Lou hesitate, Alex interceded, "Put a two-hour limit on it Lou. It's just a hike."

Against his better judgment, Lou provided the passes. "Two hours starting when you leave the gate. Got it?"

Upset by the hassle, Daniel and Lydia returned to their apartments where they found some warm clothes and filled a Thermos with hot cider from the kitchen butler. They returned to the gate thankful Alex was still on duty. He time-stamped their passes and allowed them to exit.

The couple walked through the gate, the spontaneous joy of their adventure gone.

"Make a snowman for me," Alex called.

Lydia and Daniel tramped through the three-foot snow towards the woods. When they'd walked about a mile, Lydia turned to Daniel. "I feel like a prisoner having to ask permission to take a walk."

Daniel flinched. Lydia had no idea what being a prisoner really felt like.

"We're in a high security city. Terrorists. They have to be careful of the president."

They continued to walk, each step more difficult as the heavy, wet snow packed around their hiking boots.

"Have you seen snow before, Daniel?"

"A lot of people don't know it, but there's some great skiing in Arizona. I've gone to Flagstaff and Sunrise but I've never really seen a fresh snow like this...it's like diamonds sparkling everywhere." Self-conscious about his poetic words, Daniel ran ahead, scooped up a pile of snow, rolled it into a ball and let it fly. The snowball hit Lydia in the legs.

"Oh, you want to play, do you?" She packed a snowball and belted Daniel in the back of the head.

Daniel tackled her gently, wrestling her to the ground. "You don't want to attack a Guardian. You are asking for trouble."

"Stop, stop, I surrender." Lydia lay back, enjoying each snowflake as it melted on her face. Daniel brushed the snow off her face. Then he bent over and kissed her.

Embarrassed, Lydia sat up laughing. "So you're the kind who takes advantage of a girl when her defenses are down."

Daniel pulled her up. "You got me, princess."

Breathless, Lydia said, "The snow is magic, Daniel, so natural. Even prettier than…"

"Be careful, Senator Cohen, I'm recording you." But Daniel understood what she meant. You just can't improve on nature.

He watched Lydia stare at the intricate pattern of the snowflake on her red mitten.

"They say there's no two alike," Daniel said.

Lydia looked up to see Daniel fall backward into an untouched pile of snow. He moved his arms up and down, then stood up.

"A perfect snow angel!" Lydia clapped her mittens together, delighted. Then she plunked down into the snow and did the same. Two angels, side by side.

They walked further into the woods, stopping to sit with their backs to a tree. Pouring a cup of steaming cider, Daniel looked at Lydia, her eyelashes laden with giant white snowflakes. He'd never seen anyone more beautiful.

After they finished their cider, they packed up. "We'd better get back. We don't want the Guardians hunting us," Daniel said.

Lydia pushed him playfully. "I'll sic my Guardian on them."

Suddenly sober, Daniel looked her in the eyes. "The Guardians are no joke, Lydia." He'd experienced that firsthand. And Daniel also knew they couldn't take the authority of their new world lightly either. "Just the same, we'd better show up for our two o'clock introductory class."

"Lead on. I'm right behind you, cowboy."

The pair hiked back into the golden city, changed clothes quickly, donned their blue Youth Council robes, and went directly to the Youth Council for a series on the initiatives. Daniel sat quietly making no comments, more than familiar with the initiatives and discouraged there wasn't one initiative he believed in.

As they walked out Lydia whispered, "You've been through the Ascension personally, Danny. Was it really beautiful?"

Stunned that anyone would describe the Ascension as a beautiful event, Daniel decided to end the conversation. He didn't want to discuss the Ascension. He didn't want to fight the memories it brought back.

"I'm sorry, Lydia." He walked off. Returning to his apartment, he slid his passkey into the door and sat down with his head in his hands. No matter how much he wanted to succeed in the Youth Council, mention of the initiatives—the Ascension, the Lamb's Project—brought back so many terrible memories. Despite six months at Fort Thompson, he knew he'd never get over the Ascension.

A knock on the door interrupted his thoughts. Daniel ignored it.

"Daniel, open up. I want to talk to you."

Daniel opened the door.

"What did I say? We had such a wonderful day. Tell me what's wrong. You saw the Ascension, I just wanted to know…"

Daniel cut her off. "They gas them. The people. Then they cremate the bodies and send the ashes home to the families with a letter from the president. In the letter, he calls them heroes." Daniel looked away overcome with sadness and loss.

"I didn't know," Lydia said softly. She looked shocked. "I watched it on television and it seemed like such a phenomenal thing for these people to do. I thought they were real American heroes. The event seemed so surreal and beautiful. I thought it was a wonderful initiative that would save millions and millions of health care dollars. No expensive organ transplants, heart surgeries, cancer treatments, no long-term care facilities needed…" Lydia stopped, aware of how upset her words made Daniel. "I'm sorry."

It was surreal all right, Daniel thought. He remembered the heavenly smoke machines and the chute where the bodies dropped into the crematorium. The ashes taken to the relatives were not even their loved ones…just a jar filled from the crematorium. After the event, the Guardians were assigned that duty too. He'd never forget the cries of the little children and the tears of the young woman with multiple sclerosis he'd helped out of the wheelchair. "I don't think you can understand, Lydia." Daniel took a deep breath, and then let it go. "You had to be there. They had to be your family."

"Oh, my gosh, like Auschwitz."

"What?"

"Daniel, maybe I do understand a little. My family is Jewish. My parents showed me pictures of my great grandparents. They were taken to one of the death camps, Auschwitz, and gassed during World War II. My grandfather was only ten years old."

Daniel listened, waiting for the rest of her story.

"It really affected my parents. They researched our family. My great grandpa was a professor in Austria. At first, he lost his teaching position and it was dangerous to go out on the street even for food. All Jews had to wear armbands and later they were seized in their home and taken by railcars to Auschwitz. They had numbers burned into their forearms." Tears rolled down Lydia's cheeks.

"Did your parents take the number, Lydia?"

"I don't know, Daniel. I'll find out when I go home for spring break. Knowing them, I doubt it. No Jewish person who is old will want to take any kind of number."

Lydia left and Daniel dressed for the pool. He swam, pounding the water, hoping with each stroke and kick that there would be no more initiatives like the Ascension. Fifty laps turned into sixty. The water in Daniel's lane changed colors from dark blue to green. The calmer he got, the greener the water. Anyone could tell his state of mind by looking at the water. He climbed out of the pool and toweled off, unaware that Lydia was watching him.

"Do you feel better?" she asked.

Embarrassed, Daniel shook water all over her. He didn't want her to ask him questions like that, especially in a public place. "Be careful, Miss Lydia, or you're liable to end up in the water yourself."

They might not be free to call their parents whenever they wanted to, or leave anytime they wanted to, but life inside the City of Gold was pure freedom in every other way. The president encouraged the Youth Council members to enjoy any relationship they desired whether male or female. Daniel wondered if President Blackstone and the Prophet had a special relationship with each other as neither appeared to be married.

Things were different here. Out on his balcony in the evening Daniel saw couples enjoying the hot tubs on their patios, nude. But one afternoon as he prepared to swim laps, he discovered Lydia, topless in a bikini, with some friends by the pool in an area designed with special tanning lights. Startled, he wanted to cover her up. He didn't like other guys seeing how beautiful she was. Lydia smiled an innocent smile and beckoned him over, pulling a towel up over her body.

"Isn't it wonderful how free it is?" she asked him. "Nothing's wrong here. We can enjoy life as it was meant to be enjoyed. In my home everything is so private, so covered up, so not talked about." She stopped, seeing the look on his face. "What's the matter, Danny?"

" I don't like the looks those guys are giving you."

"Don't pay any attention to them. They probably just want to get on my calendar."

"You don't have a calendar, do you? You aren't having sex with…"

"Why, Danny, are you jealous? Do you care? We're young, beautiful, and they've given us everything to enjoy. Isn't it wrong not to enjoy our new life?"

"I don't know, Lydia. All I know is that I don't want a bunch of guys coming on to you." Daniel got up and dove back into the pool. He reached the end of the lane where a lean guy with dark curly hair was sitting with his legs in the water.

"I've been watching you swim," the guy said. His eyes roved down Daniel's body muscle by muscle. "If you're interested, I'll be in Suite 217 in about an hour. See you then. The name's Conrad."

Daniel stared at Conrad as he moved away. Nothing in his life prepared him for this kind of living. It repulsed him. Sports had sheltered him and he didn't realize how out of sync he was with the rest of the world. A lot of guys in his school had one-night stands and never even said hello to the girl the next day. Sex was considered a casual event, but it wasn't to Daniel. Finding a special girl for his life was almost sacred. Daniel wanted an old-fashioned marriage like his parents and grandparents. He wiped the water out of his eyes and looked at Lydia who was now surrounded by six guys.

Daniel left without saying goodbye.

Later that night as he watched a movie, he heard a knock. Opening the door, he found Lydia dressed in shorts and a clean white short-sleeved shirt that showed off her tan. "Can I come in?" she asked.

Daniel opened the door and motioned to the couch. Lydia slid her arms around Daniel's neck. His heart hammered but he continued to stare at the TV. Lydia began to unbutton her blouse. Daniel watched her, then against every emotion in his body, he buttoned her up again.

"I don't understand, Danny. Don't you want me?"

"Lydia, I think you should go."

"Talk to me, Danny. I know you like me. What's wrong?"

Daniel stood up and paced in front of the couch. "I just want sex to mean something. You know? I want to be with one special person. I don't want to share that person with other guys or women. I'm not like that, Lydia. Someday, I want to find someone to love and spend my life with." Daniel hadn't looked at Lydia since he'd begun his speech. He expected her to laugh at him but when he looked at her, she wasn't laughing.

"Am I that person for you, Danny?"

"I don't know. I thought, maybe…"

"But now you don't?"

"Lydia, it would break my heart to have a relationship with you and to have to share you with anyone who came along. Do you understand? I can't do that."

Lydia breathed a sigh of relief. She cuddled up next to him and settled down to watch the movie. "Let's take it slow and see if we've found something special. Deal?"

He answered her with a kiss.

Chapter Five

Sebastian Cramer wrapped the tattered blanket around his shoulders and hunkered down under the underpass, wishing he had a cardboard box to shelter him from the blowing dust. He studied the people huddled under the bridge with him: a muscular, middle-aged man in an old Diamondback's jacket; a Mexican family huddled around a small fire trying to keep warm in the cold night air; an old grandmother wrapped in a poncho running a rosary through her fingers, silently praying as she rocked back and forth; a long-haired, teenage guy with a guitar played softly, and a girl who looked like she might be his sister sang along under her breath as she hugged an old golden retriever. *Why were they here? What was their story?* Sebastian assumed it had to do with not taking the number to buy and sell or they were homeless for some other reason. People conserved their energy. It was too much trouble to make conversation. And if they were like him, they probably didn't want to share private stories.

A little two-year-old boy, barefoot and dressed in tiny worn jeans, wandered over to Sebastian. His brown eyes blinked as he held out a crust of bread. Sebastian looked over at the mother, her dull hair pulled back in a ponytail, surrounded by two other small, dirty children holding tightly to ragged, stuffed bears. Smiling she said, "Please take it, sir, I'm trying to teach them that we must care for one another. God has provided for us today."

Sebastian took the piece of bread, even though he felt irritated by her irrational love for this God who'd betrayed them all. He watched the little boy toddle back to his mother. She tucked a child under each arm to keep them warm, leaning against the concrete underpass.

This was Sebastian's third night under the bridge. He watched the dwellers share everything—coats, cardboard boxes, and even their bread. He glanced at the boy who'd given him the crust, now sleeping soundly in his mother's lap. *How could you let these little children live like this? Where is your heart, God?*

Folding up his sport coat, he placed it under his head, covering himself with the old blanket. He closed his eyes listening to the cars thundering on the 101 above them. How many times had he driven his silver Prius over this stretch of road? He longed for his old life, life before his wife Callie died; a life that included hot showers and clean white shirts, coffee from Starbucks, and a paycheck. But most of all, Callie.

Nervous, Sebastian kept his eyes focused on the highway above the bridge. He wished the young man with the guitar would quit playing and the babies would stop crying—dead giveaways to the Guardian patrols who canvassed the area. Tomorrow he'd try to find a new spot, one without cigarette butts, beer cans, and javelina droppings. The past three nights the bridge dwellers had been safe from the Guardians' raids, but tonight felt different.

Sebastian Cramer, PhD, entered a nightmare when his wife Callie was diagnosed with ovarian cancer. He hated what the disease did to her body and he hated God for allowing his beautiful Callie to die in such a horrible way. But he'd lost more than his job taking care of Callie. He'd lost all track of time…It had been worth it though. He still thought that. Callie was the most precious thing in his life.

Despite the fact that he'd worked consistently, saved money, and invested wisely, all his finances were confiscated by the government when he missed the deadline to join One World Finances. The same week he buried Callie, Sebastian lost his home. Nothing remained of his old life. His effort each day was finding food to stay alive and finding a place to sleep where the Guardians wouldn't arrest him. And... he really didn't know how to do either very well.

Sebastian picked up a leftover *Wall Street Journal*, the last remaining newspaper, scanning the headlines in the darkening dusk. *What was happening to the United States?* From his point of view under the bridge, change for many had not been good. *Where would he end up?* He shivered, longing for a hot coffee. Tomorrow, he'd visit the restaurant he and Callie considered "their" place and see if his friend Chef Thomas would give him some food. Tonight, the little boy's bread would have to be enough.

Rick Hathaway fit well into his new MP Guardian life. The last he'd heard, his old partner Daniel Jordan was still in Fort Thompson having his brain fried but Daniel's loss was his gain. Transferred to the Guardian MPs, Rick now tracked down dissidents for the administration—a full-time job—delivering them to Luke Air Force base for the dissi-dent prison in Kansas.

Rick and his partner rounded up outspoken media pun-dits, conservative politicians, religious ministers, and the ever-growing number of Christians and Jews who refused to take the number to buy and sell.

Tonight, instead of frequenting his neighborhood night spot for happy hour, Rick decided to make one last run on the freeway underpasses where homeless families tended to sleep at night. The administration kept track of the number of dissidents rounded up by each Guardian. He and his partner cruised the 101 hoping to score big. Every dissident rounded up put Rick that much closer to the real assignment he hoped for…MP duty at the dissident prison in Kansas and then an assignment to the Guardian Corps in the City of Gold.

"Stop here, Freddie." Rick was right. Even from a dis-tance, he could see homeless people huddled under the underpass. He signaled his partner and they moved forward crouching low. He checked his taser, flicked the switch off, and replaced it in his holster. "Use the ultraviolet light to check for their number. Whoever is without, comes with us." Freddy moved around and Rick took out his smartphone recording Freddy's first arrest of the homeless on video.

Rick prodded the man in the baseball jacket. Shoving the man's sleeve up Rick discovered he had no number. "Let's go." He kicked the boy with the guitar. "Stop that lame music, kid." Realizing the kid didn't look twenty-one nor did his sister, he moved on. "C'mon Grandma, show me your arm." The old lady pushed her sleeve up and the ultraviolet light confirmed she had no number either. "Bring your rosary and let's go. You can pray for yourself in prison."

Rick spotted two families with small children. He signaled Freddie to leave them alone but the flashlights woke them and their frightened crying screeched on Rick's nerves. No provision existed for kids at Leavenworth. Kids were trouble. Leave them alone on the streets and it reflected poorly on the administration. They finished rounding up the people without numbers and shoved them into the van.

"Good haul, huh Freddy?"

Sebastian's intuition had been right. Tonight was different. Tonight, his freedom was lost. Well, at least in prison there'd be a bed and food. Reluctantly, he got in the van with the unfortunate group caught by the Guardians who deposited them at the base.

Rick returned to his condo. Before crashing, he checked the messages on his communicator. CALL HQ, ASAP.

The next morning as Rick sat waiting in the outer office of his supervisor, he glanced at the office media center. Pictures of the midnight arrest of the vagrants under the bridge flashed across the screen. He appreciated the fact that a reporter picked up the story he'd sent via his smartphone.

The door to the captain's office opened and a voice called, "Come in, Rick. Good work last night."

"Thank you, sir."

"I've been impressed with your dedication lately. Been studying your file. You have the highest number of dissident arrests among the Guardian MPs. I want to discuss an opening at Leavenworth. Are you interested?"

Rick's ego inflated. One step closer to his dream goal. "Yes, sir."

"Afraid the nightlife is rather limited, but the salary increase is substantial."

Rick laughed. "I think I'll survive, Captain, and yes... I'm your man."

Relieved, Captain Grant shook Rick's hand. "Can you be ready by this weekend?"

Jerry Grunwald despised working for the Prophet. Once a week, he transported dissidents to Leavenworth prison from Central Base Headquarters in Phoenix. At first it was religious fanatics, men and women who wouldn't take the number and were now homeless and starving. He also took the dissidents who rebelled against the initiatives. He'd swear that last week he'd taken the unconscious guy who was supposed to be blown up by terrorists…a doc. Jerry thought he might have been the doc who headed up the Center for New Age Medicine in Phoenix.

He looked over the new crop of dissidents waiting their fate in the airport at Luke, his eyes drawn to a tall man giving his seat to an old woman with a rosary. Dressed in a navy blue sport coat, soiled white shirt and tan chinos, the man stood out. Jerry wondered what caused the "Sport Coat" to be picked up with the homeless under the bridge.

He counted twenty people he'd have to transport to Leavenworth. His back ached and he wished he could get some help for the runs he would be making on his next job delivering wooden caskets. *What if he took on one of these homeless as a helper?* He studied the man who'd caught his attention. Underneath the outer layer of grime, Sport Coat appeared healthy and muscular. Surely, he hadn't been homeless long. Jerry needed extra muscles. His old body was bruised and beaten up. Dragging cargo on and off Old

Glory to the City of Gold and Leavenworth prison these last six months had taken its toll. Jerry tapped the guy on the shoulder. He turned, and Jerry noted the sadness in his eyes. "You interested in three squares for some work on my runs?"

Sebastian looked Jerry over. "Three squares?" He wasn't sure what the old pilot meant.

"You know, three meals a day. Work for food. I need help loading and unloading."

Sebastian glanced at the old plane, considering. "Throw in a bunk and you got a helper."

"You understand you were headed for the dissident prison at Leavenworth? Let me warn you, buddy. That is the last place you want to bed down."

Sebastian looked over the old pilot, noting the name on his coveralls. "Thanks, Jerry."

Chapter Six

President Blackstone pushed the communicator signaling the Prophet. "Do you have time for a conference?"

"Yes, of course." The dark form of the vice president appeared at the door of the president's office. Why Justin Prophet always dressed in black except for his silver tie was a mystery to the president. His dark complexion and oiled black hair gave him the appearance of the mafia. Well, perhaps in a sense, he was the president's own representative of the dark side. The president flipped on the GNN and pointed to the explosion. "My friend, Dr. Hart?"

"Dr. Hart is no longer a problem."

"The car bombing was terrorists? Or are we the terrorists?"

The Prophet smiled. "It's probably better if you don't know the details."

"He's dead?"

"No, let's say he's on ice."

"The man in the car bombing?"

"A homeless person."

The president decided not to interrogate the Prophet further. He'd given the Prophet total control of the dissidents. They'd agreed that no one—whether media, misguided civil rights advocates, the religious right, professors, or lawyers—should derail the new initiatives. Omega I would not interfere with the Prophet's plans for the dissidents. He was surprised that his friend Dr. Greg Hart lasted so long.

"Dr. Hart did an excellent job setting up the Center for New Age Medicine and the Ascension," said the president.

"Yes, too bad he decided to become Mother Teresa."

Greg Hart watched a black spider work its way up the wall of the crumbling concrete block cell. *Where was he and how long had he been here?* His head ached from whatever drugs they'd shot into him. *Could this be an old military prison?* The gray concrete block cell bore marks of past inmates. He studied the wall before him. Scratched on the stones, days and names were recorded. He shivered in the cold and damp.

The spider reached the top and began to spin a web secreting a fragile thread which he wove into his web. Nature programmed the spider for its work of staying alive. Hart watched as a fly flew innocently into the lacy web. He and the fly had something in common. When Greg created the Center for New Age Medicine, he hoped to be on the cutting edge of science able to help millions. A dream come true. Like the fly, he entered the president's plan caught in a web of darkness he'd never anticipated. From his wonderful clinic, heinous initiatives denying the huge older population health care—and eventually selection for the Ascension— replaced the health care and surgeries that could have made their lives better. Greg was guilty of the murder of innocents.

Despite his moment of truth and decision to do what he could to save the condemned by performing life-saving surgeries and sending a few to his ranch in Mexico, Greg felt guilty. *Was that why he hadn't heeded his nurse's warnings to leave the Center for New Age Medicine?*

A key in the lock interrupted his thoughts. A Guardian MP signaled him to follow. Seeing the Guardian caused Dr. Hart to wonder what happened to the young Guardian he'd used to drive patients and equipment to Rancho Christo. The last he'd heard from Daniel Jordan's partner was that Daniel was "having his brain fried." Could they have traced the doctor's activities through Daniel? Or was it more likely that one of his fellow surgeons exposed him. Perhaps he'd never know.

"Follow me."

What did the administration hope to gain by bringing him to this dismal, God-forsaken prison? He'd tell them nothing that could endanger those he'd helped or his nurse, Nan. The guard opened a door to an interrogation room. A light bulb dangled from the ceiling casting an eerie shadow on the wall. A lone metal chair, looking like the old electric chairs used to end prisoners' lives, was the only thing in the room. Greg decided to stand. A voice came through a loud-speaker but no person came with it.

"Good afternoon, doctor. Please take a seat. I have a few questions to ask you."

"I'd prefer to stand."

"It isn't your preference we're interested in, doctor. Sit down."

Greg sat in the uncomfortable metal chair. As soon as he sat down, metal clamps exploded across his legs and thighs.

"Now that's better, isn't it? Are you comfortable? Just a few simple questions, and then you can return to your room. You are Dr. Greg Hart of the Center for New Age Medicine in Phoenix?"

"Not any longer."

"I would advise you to cooperate with us, doctor. Let's start again. You designed and created the Center for New Age Medicine in Phoenix. A yes or no will be sufficient."

"Yes."

"You were employed by the administration for three years?"

"Yes."

"During that time you prepared and evaluated people for the Ascension?"

"Yes. Unfortunately, many people died because of me."

"So you decided to take on a little side business, isn't that so?"

"I don't understand."

"How many life-saving surgeries did you perform, doctor?"

"I didn't count them."

"I'll ask you again. Be careful what you answer this time."

Greg said nothing. A minute went by and then a charge of electricity jolted him, tearing through his muscles. He bit his lip.

"Let's try that question again. How many life-saving surgeries did you perform illegally at the Center for New Age Medicine?"

Greg remained silent. This time the charge ricocheted up his spine into his brain, knocking him unconscious. As his head rolled forward, the clamps released and Greg pitched forward, landing unconscious on the bloodstained stone floor. When he awoke, the light bulb was swaying and Greg felt limp from the electric voltage. Brushing his hand across his eyes, he felt something sticky and wet. His hand was covered with blood. The fall had broken his nose and his head ached from hitting the stone floor. He crawled over to the wall and leaned against it. So…this is what life would be like now.

The Prophet stood up and stretched. He switched off the intercom to the interrogation room. He enjoyed his job. *Well, doctor, we shall see how long it take you to cooperate. I have the feeling you will give us the information we seek or die in*

your efforts to remain silent. Perhaps a few days without food
or water will encourage you to share your wisdom with us.

The Prophet left the prison and boarded the helicopter back to the City of Gold where he would conduct the first Youth Council meeting. The Prophet had handpicked his pilot. The man was a topnotch ace with an elderly mother, old enough to be put in the Ascension. The pilot was useful and his mother was the best insurance the Prophet had to keep his mouth shut.

"Good evening, Jerry."

Chapter Seven

President Blackstone signaled the vice president to join him. "Justin, are you ready to become a shepherd for these young Council members?"

The vice president flinched. He hated it when the president used Biblical pictures. "Yes, but I prefer to think of myself as their guide."

"Are we clear on what we hope to achieve with this group of young adults?"

"Absolutely clear. We are to desensitize them to the world from which they've come and surround them with a life so rich and free that they think of us as their true home."

"And every initiative we dream up as created by wise and educated people who are trying to make a better world for the majority," said the president.

"America was founded on individual freedom; they must learn to think in terms of what is good for the many."

"Changing their attitude about the Constitution is crucial. Are we agreed?"

"Of course," said the Prophet. "Living in a futuristic city, they must want a new design—a constitution for the times. We are no longer a nation under God; we are a nation under the globe."

"Well spoken."

Daniel and Lydia entered the Youth Council eager to meet the Prophet who would conduct the group. Unsure what the Council was created for, Daniel waited in hopes the Prophet would make that clear. As a Guardian his job had been to implement the new initiatives. Initiatives he did not believe in. Initiatives that took away individual rights and had hurt his family and many old and ill people. Still, Daniel hoped for a new life. He looked at Lydia so eager and enthusiastic. Still suspicious of the administration who created all the change, Daniel was on guard.

The Prophet sat alone at the table for five staring at the Council members as they entered. The room soon filled up and the Prophet banged his gavel.

A message appeared on the overhead screen. "We'll begin our sessions with a dedication. You will read out loud the purpose and goals of the Youth Council." A collective quiet fell over the assembly as the students digested the slogan before them. "All rise," said the Prophet.

The group rose and read in unison: "As a Youth Council member, I will be true to the goals and initiatives set forth by the government of the United States of America. I give my unconditional allegiance to the president. I will be a faithful and loyal member of the President's Youth Council. I will think only of what is best for my country and for the future."

The Prophet again sounded his gavel and everyone sat down. Smiling, he called the Council to order. Daniel's heart began to beat rapidly. Chills accompanied the racing heartbeat and an uneasiness settled over him.

"Let's begin with your impressions of the City of Gold. Stand in place and give your thoughts."

The girl from Rhode Island stood. "I think it's the most beautiful city anyone could imagine. I'm thrilled to be here."

Michigan stood. "The engineers who designed the dome outdid themselves, making us not only safe, but giving us perfect weather and temperatures every day. Sure beats the blizzards we get in winter."

Colorado. "My family is a little rigid. I enjoy the freedom to live without so many rules."

Lydia joined the accolades for the city. "Not only is it the most beautiful city in the world, sir, but I appreciate the Council members you've chosen. We're meeting such high quality friends." She sat down looking over at Daniel.

"As Youth Council members you will eventually be ambassadors. We plan to send you back to visit high schools in your home state. Your job will be to hold special assemblies explaining the history of the initiatives. But first, you will have intensive classes to educate each of you on the history and purpose of each change and new initiative. Most of you are familiar with the first initiative, the Ascension, in which our senior citizens gave their lives for the good of the country. Not only did they bring honor to their families but they may very well have saved our country from economic disaster. As a result of the experiment in Phoenix, there will be Ascension opportunities in each state.

"Since you've all recently graduated from high school, one of your tasks will be to design initiatives for the education system that can be submitted to the Council of Twelve and the Board of Governors for their consideration. The Youth Council will vote on the initiatives submitted and the

Council members receiving the most votes will be elected president and vice president. The winners will receive a travel voucher for a trip of their choice. Are there any questions?"

Lydia stood.

"Chair recognizes the Council member from California."

"Sir, I think it would be helpful as ambassadors to have a video we can present to the high schools we speak to, showing the students how the initiatives will work. A national promotion perhaps."

The Prophet's eyes glistened. "May I have your name, Councilwoman?"

Lydia blushed. "Lydia Cohen, sir."

"An excellent idea, Ms. Cohen. Perhaps you would like to organize a team to produce this video when the initiatives have been selected."

Lydia and Daniel left the Youth Council meeting excited with the prospect of the work that lie ahead.

"Girl, you were amazing! No wonder California sent you to represent their state. Your project already has the approval and eyes of the Prophet."

"Would you consider being on my team, Danny?"

Daniel hesitated, wanting to say yes, but not sure if he could still follow through with the project that seemed important to him.

"Did you have something you really wanted to pursue?"

"Yeah, I guess I do. Technology is taking a toll on teens' physical health. Not only are they couch potatoes but the obsession to text is totally out of hand. I'd like to see each student assigned a physical trainer who would design an exercise program appropriate for them."

"Then that's what you should do," said Lydia. "Would you like to help with the national promotion part-time?"

Lydia was unbelievable. Her idea would probably get her elected president of the Council but she was sport enough to see Daniel's passion. He breathed a sigh of relief.

"Of course, I'll help."

"How would you pay for the trainers, Daniel?" she asked. "The schools are pretty strapped for money."

"True, but think of the difference healthy bodies would make on health costs as people grow older. Maybe the money could come from a federal agency or a grant from the World Health Organization."

Chapter Eight

Daniel presented his program in one of the next sessions. The majority applauded the idea of trainers designing an individual regime for each student. Daniel clinched their approval by making a PowerPoint video showing the program in action. Even the Prophet got on board stating he would show Daniel how to present a request for a grant from the World Health Organization as a model for a global program. Both Daniel and Lydia's ideas put them out front in the race for the sought-after travel vacation. Caught up in the work of the Youth Council, they found little time to be together.

One night when Lydia's team had a planning session, Daniel decided to jog around the city. He breathed in the scent of the night-blooming jasmine, enjoying the moonlight on the waterways. The sound of water falling over rocks added a rhythm to his jog. As he approached the golden statue, he stopped to rest on a park bench. The statue was a likeness of Omega I, forty feet high. *Could the gold color be real gold?* Slowly, Daniel moved closer to the statue to get a better view. The statue appeared to have been dipped in pure liquid gold or had the entire figure been cast in gold?

"So Daniel, you wish to know me?"

Daniel stood still, not speaking.

"I know you. You are a doubter. You have been a prisoner at Fort Thompson."

Shaken, Daniel stepped back trying to get out of the range of the statue. *How could it possibly know about Fort Thompson? Even the president didn't know about Fort Thompson. Had someone programmed the statue? But who?*

Fear overtook Daniel. He ran, trying to outdistance the panic the statue triggered. Beads of sweat broke out on his forehead. He had so hoped...wanted so badly to start a new life. His work had gone well at the Youth Council. Awaking from the dream of a new life, he found himself still in a terrible nightmare. *How could he forget the Ascension and the Lamb's Project? Did the statue communicate its interac-*

tions? Would someone learn his secret? He was afraid to go back to his rooms. He knocked on Lydia's door.

She opened the door, a look of surprise on her face. "Do you want to come in?"

"No, could you put on something and come out?"

"Danny, what's wrong? You look upset." Lydia threw on some sweats and joined him.

"Lydia there are some things I want you to know..." Daniel poured out his story about Fort Thompson and the Guardians until the pain was gone. "I know you probably can't buy any of this but the statue..."

"The golden statue?"

"Somehow, it reads your mind and it knows all this."

"Daniel, when I told you I thought it talked to me, you said the statue was just a clever invention, programmed with information about each of us."

"No, it's more than that. It called me a doubter. Said I'd been a prisoner and then mentioned Fort Thompson. No one here except you knows that, not even the president. Captain Taylor told me he sent only my Guardian and high school records."

"I don't know what to say, Daniel. I can see why you'd be suspicious with all you've been through. Can't you just stay away from the statue? You like our work on the Council, don't you? The Council accepted your plan for the personal trainers." She kissed him lightly on the forehead. "It's just too soon; you aren't healed enough. Everything will be all right. You need some sleep. Me, too. Everything will seem better tomorrow, you'll see."

Was he paranoid? Had his experiences made him so suspicious that he was inventing problems? Why had he downloaded all his fears on Lydia?

Chapter Nine

Every day Daniel expected someone to take him to the office of the Prophet for interrogation. The golden statue's knowledge of his time at Fort Thompson unnerved him, and he avoided it, concentrating on his coming spring break. Daniel hadn't seen his family since October, seven months ago.

A few days before the break, Daniel found a roundtrip airline ticket on his desk—American World Airlines—a commercial flight, not a military one. Did this mean he was no longer under suspicion? The note accompanying the tickets informed him the administration had notified his parents of his flight and arrival times. He was going home!

That evening after dinner, he walked Lydia to her apartment. "I'll miss you, Lydia. I wish there was some way you could meet my family. I know you'd like them."

"I feel the same way, Danny, but you haven't seen your family for so long, don't you think you need to be alone with them? If I were there, you'd be paying attention to me, not them. Much as I'd like to meet them, I think you need this time with your family."

"I guess you're right..." He pulled Lydia close to him brushing her face with his lips... "just as long as you don't have an old flame at home."

"You don't mind if I tell my mother I have a boyfriend, do you?"

"Not if you're telling the truth."

Daniel's flight left mid-morning. He packed his duffle, showered, and dressed carefully in the navy wool blazer, gray slacks, and red tie customary for Council members. One thing about Omega I, he wanted his Council to look first class. Daniel was also flying first class with all the perks.

Memories returned of the night the Guardians came for him, pounding on the door at midnight, rough hands pulling him out of bed and shoving him downstairs, no one understanding what Daniel was accused of or where the Guardians were taking him. Finally, Daniel learned that it was his mother who reported him to Captain Stern.

In Fort Thompson Daniel felt violated, forced to undergo laser brain treatments and drug therapy. He'd nearly lost his mind. His mom didn't know what she was doing to Daniel by reporting him to the captain but Daniel held no anger toward her. He hoped his dad hadn't been too hard on her. It was over now. They'd be all right once they saw him healthy and happy.

Daniel climbed aboard the plane and stashed his duffle bag in the overhead storage. The captain announced his flight plan while Daniel buckled his seat belt. He looked around the compartment—mostly people conducting business on communicators or reading e-books. Taking a seat next to a white-haired senior citizen already dozing, he watched the plane rise into the sunset.

As the plane descended, Daniel recognized the Verde River winding through the desert, then caught sight of Camelback Mountain and Arizona State University as the plane glided into Sky Harbor Airport. On landing, he down-loaded his duffel and exited the plane. At the security checkpoint, he spotted Penny waving and pulling their parents toward him.

"Family!" He put his arms around all three at once which made Harry laugh.

"Oh, Daniel, you haven't changed a bit," cooed his mother.

"C'mon, guys, let's get some Mexican."

"But we have a reservation for Joey's," Judith interrupted.

"Please Mom, I missed the desert. Just Mexican tonight, okay?"

Harry smiled. "Jump in the car and we'll take you by the college to Chili's." He turned to Judith. "Call Joey's and reschedule for another night."

Full of questions Penny asked, "Meet any new friends, Danny?"

"I met a girl...a beautiful girl from San Diego, Lydia Cohen."

"Isn't that a Jewish name, Daniel? I'm surprised a Jewish girl was chosen for the Youth Council," said his mother.

"She's beautiful and probably the smartest one in the Council," Daniel replied.

"Tell us about her, Danny. What's she like?" said Penny.

"She's dark-haired...lavender eyes...warm...funny... fun."

"Nobody has lavender eyes, Danny."

"Well, they change, Penny, sometimes gray, sometimes blue, sometimes lavender."

Penny shook her head. "Does she ride horses?"

"I don't know, Pen. I never thought to ask her."

"Daniel...we live on a horse ranch."

"I know, but we just had other things to talk about."

Harry drove to the restaurant dreading the fact that Judith controlled all the money now and ashamed she'd pay the bill for their outing, the price he paid for refusing to take the number. He intended to keep the vow he'd made to honor his parents no matter how uncomfortable Judith made him feel about the money.

Probably because of the Fort Thompson debacle, Judith said little about paying for everything. In return Harry held his tongue about Judith's call to Captain Stern. Harry still didn't trust her. *Should he warn Daniel to be careful what he said in front of his mother? Why did Judith have to be the enemy?* Maybe in some backward way, Judith's betrayal actually propelled Daniel into a better life. He hoped so. Daniel appeared happy.

Daniel slipped away from the group, entering his old bedroom. He rifled through his drawers until he found... jeans. He hung his jacket and slacks on a hanger and donned the familiar washed out denims, a favorite T-shirt, and his old cowboy boots. Now...he was home.

Judith collapsed in a chair beside the natural stone fireplace in the great room, completely vindicated that she'd called Captain Stern. If she hadn't, Daniel would not be in the Youth Council. He'd still be a Guardian. Tears of relief welled up in her eyes. Since the day the MPs came for Daniel, an icy wall had separated her and Harry. Penny knew of course, but both she and Harry pretended everything was fine—two actors in a bad play. Maybe now things could get back to normal except for Harry refusing to take the number and the problem it made for her. Judith just wanted her home to feel comfortable again, the icy walls to melt.

After supper, the next evening, the family moved into the great room. "Tell us about your assignment, son," Harry began.

"Well, I thought I was going to Washington, D.C. where all the government stuff was but when I looked out of the helicopter, it was landing through the dome of the most futuristic city I've ever seen. It's called the City of Gold."

Harry was puzzled. He hadn't seen anything about a futuristic city on the news. "The City of Gold?"

"That's what they call it, Dad. Omega I designed the city and moved the Council of Twelve, the Board of Governors and the Youth Council there. He splits his time between D.C. and the City of Gold."

"What does it look like, Danny?" asked Penny.

"They built the city under a dome to create a greenhouse effect. The temperature never fluctuates; it's always in the high seventies. The pilot who flew me to the new capital delivered a plane full of exotic flowers at the same time. I suspect the dome may be antimissile to protect the president and the lawmakers."

"Where is this city?" Harry asked.

"It's in Kansas, far enough from the coast to intercept any missiles. The city is entirely blue glass with its own satellite studio, a revolving restaurant, housing, recreation, and government facilities." Daniel painted a picture of the futuristic city but avoided telling his family about the golden statue of Omega I and the free lifestyle. His suspicions of the administration caused him to be cautious. He decided he'd protect his family and himself better if they weren't upset, especially his mother. "The Prophet told us that the Youth Council installation will be televised worldwide. They plan to unveil the city at the same time. The security is high—only those who work in the city are allowed in so far. It is beautiful. I hope you get a chance to visit."

Spring break nearly over, Daniel checked in with Hal at the Guardian Training School and drove his motorcycle down to Tucson to spend an evening with Joey. He said little about his own year but listened avidly as both boys related theirs.

Before returning to the City of Gold, Daniel had one more thing to do—ride up to the caves. While a prisoner at Fort Thompson, he'd thought a lot about the contents of the wooden box Grandpa left him. Several questions bothered Daniel. He'd seen a reference to someone called "the lawless man." Did Grandpa mark passages about him? And what exactly did that mean?

On his last visit to the caves, he'd read only about the life of the holy man, Jesus. Why did Grandpa want Daniel to know about Him? Was it because Grandpa thought they were getting into the times the old Bible spoke of in the future? What did the book say? And...why was a map included? If he rode up to the caves and back in the same day, he'd have a nice ride on Sandy, eat lunch, dig up the box, and answer the nagging questions.

The next day, Daniel accepted a lunch from his mom and saddled Sandy for the ride to the caves. Once there, Daniel led the horse to the river for a drink, tied him on a mesquite branch, and dug up the wooden box. He lifted the old Bible out of the plastic bag and looked through its pages.

The next marker was in 2 Thessalonians. He noticed a section title: *The Man of Lawlessness*, and read, *"Concerning the coming of our Lord Jesus Christ and our being gathered to him, we ask you not to become alarmed. That day will not come until the rebellion occurs and the man of lawlessness is revealed."* Daniel scanned further. *"The coming of the lawless one will be in accordance with the work of Satan displayed in all kinds of counterfeit miracles, signs and wonders and in every sort of evil that deceives those who are perishing."*

Daniel sucked in his breath and reread the words. The man who wrote this, Paul, was saying that Jesus, the holy man was coming to earth again. Wow. So that's why Grandpa marked the story of Jesus' life. He wanted Daniel to know about Him. What were counterfeiting miracles? And what would the evil man counterfeit? The sentence about the signs and wonders could definitely apply to the golden statue.

He took out the map noting the letter "R" marked in several states. On the bottom of the map, Daniel noticed a note: "R"—safe houses for the remnant of true believers. So the map marked towns where the followers of the old ways could go. He looked closer—none in Phoenix but one close to Kansas City—a couple in Canada. Perhaps Rancho Christo was one of these safe houses even though it wasn't on this map. But why did Grandpa include the map? Did he think Daniel or his family would need it?

He picked up the white stone, with the dove etched on it. What was its purpose? Slipping the white stone into his jeans pocket, he placed the old book and map back in the wooden box and reburied it, wishing he could read more about Jesus and about the man of lawlessness. Could it be that the lawless man would not respect the laws of the land but would create his own? Daniel closed his eyes. "Thanks, Grandpa, for trying to warn me." He rode back to the ranch, glad he'd met Grandpa's God despite the brutal months at the Fort.

Later that night Daniel found his dad in the workshop.

"Daniel, sit. Has the entire government moved to the City of Gold?"

"I think all business is conducted in the City of Gold. The president flies to Washington to meet foreign dignitaries. Nothing on the media about the new capital?"

"No, son, nothing at all; that's what surprises me."

"Dad, not to change the subject, but are you going to sell my motorcycle?"

"Let's wait and see. Time enough to sell it, if you can't use it."

Daniel was relieved even though he'd never be able to use it in the City of Gold.

"Did you take the number, Dad?"

"No, I won't be taking it, Danny. It's my way of honoring Grandpa. How 'bout you? Will they make you take it?"

"I have to take it when I turn 21. Most of the Youth Council is under 21 and, so far, everything is furnished. I'm like you, Dad. I don't think I can take it."

Harry looked up. Daniel faced a dilemma. If he refused to take the number, he would be sent to a dissident prison. If he took the number, according to Harry's father, his soul would be lost. Unlike Judith who thought her dreams for Daniel were coming true, Harry saw massive storm clouds in Daniel's future.

Chapter Ten

Daniel stared at the bank of clouds on the horizon. Lightning zigzagged across the sky. The storm brewing between his parents diffused when they saw he was happy and liked his work. Getting away from the City of Gold for spring break renewed and relaxed him, although he didn't know whether Dad would ever be able to trust his mom again after she'd betrayed Daniel by calling Captain Stern. Unsure himself, Daniel steered away from any private conversations with his mother. No one asked questions or discussed his time in Fort Thompson. Now Daniel was eager to return to the City of Gold to be with Lydia again.

After the flight to the Kansas City airport, Daniel hunted for the special shuttle to the City of Gold. The bus dropped him outside the gates of the city. Alex was manning the security station. "Hey, Al, how's it goin?"

"Everything's cool in paradise," Al replied.

Daniel stopped by Lydia's suite, knocking lightly on her door. The door flew open and Lydia jumped on him giving him a big bear hug. He set her feet on the floor and led her to the couch. "Does everyone get that greeting?" he chuckled.

"Only you, Danny."

"That's good. Everything all right at home?"

Lydia lowered her eyes unsure whether to confide in Daniel. "It was hard, Danny. My parents didn't take the number. They told me as Jews they still remembered when Hitler made the Jews wear armbands and burned numbers into their arms. So...they don't have access to their bank accounts anymore. They own their house and paid their bills ahead. They have plenty of food stored up, a small garden for vegetables and a freezer of meat. I'm really worried about them. They told me that the past doesn't need to be my problem. I am free to make my own decision about the number. My birthday will be coming in a few months. I don't know what to do."

"My dad didn't take the number, and I'm not sure I can take it either, Lydia."

"But Daniel, once we turn twenty-one we can't live here and be on the Youth Council without it."

Daniel nodded, "I know. I've thought a lot about it. My mother took the number so right now my family is all right."

"But why wouldn't your dad take it, Daniel. What reason did he have?"

"My grandparents were Christians. They came into Phoenix in the hot summer to show us what the Bible said about taking the number. Do you know the Bible actually foretold a time when people in the world would be asked to take a number to buy or sell? The Bible also said if anyone took the number they would lose the right to go to heaven."

"Do you believe that, Danny?"

"I haven't decided, but yes, I think maybe I do."

Lydia looked away. Her parents left her free to take the number but if Daniel didn't take it when he turned twenty-one, he would lose his life here in the City of Gold. She wasn't sure she could do that. She was having wonderful success in the Youth Council. Well, they had some time, hopefully enough to convince Daniel.

"What else did you do while you were home?" Daniel asked thinking it was time to change the subject.

"I watched some movies with my parents, walked the beach, and read an old fiction series. Did you ever hear of the Hunger Games? It was about a couple like us living in an unknown land, maybe the U.S. after a nuclear attack. How was your family?"

"My sister, Penny, was mad because I didn't bring you home. Her first question was, 'Does she ride horses?' Funny, I guess I never asked you. Do you?"

"Am I rejected if I say no?" She ruffled Daniel's hair. "I've ridden a few times on the beach. Not like you all must ride."

"Okay, you're not rejected. But the next question is a big one, have you ever ridden on a motorcycle?"

Lydia's mouth dropped open. "You're kidding, right?"

"As a matter of fact, I own one. I call him the Black Mustang. He saved my life more than once when I was in the Guardians."

Lydia shook her head. "You are a real mystery, Daniel. My parents were trying to get used to the idea of me dating a cowboy. I don't dare tell them the cowboy rides motorcycles. They'd have you in a gang."

The teasing stopped. Daniel pulled her close to him. "I missed you."

"Me, too."

"Shall we go to dinner?"

"How 'bout we sit on the verandah with some stuff from the kitchen butler."

"My kind of girl," Daniel whispered.

The next day as they were walking, they approached the golden statue and Daniel took Lydia's hand, swinging her away from its reach.

Lydia challenged him. "Are you still avoiding the statue?"

Daniel looked uncomfortable. He didn't know how to tell her he actually felt a strong sense of evil coming from it.

"I think I'll have to get the number, Danny. I don't want to risk my life here in the City of Gold."

Daniel froze. "When is your birthday?"

"In a few months."

"Promise me something, Lydia."

"Sure, Danny."

"Promise you won't take the number ahead of time. Let's think about it." *But what good would it do to think about it if Lydia doesn't believe in God or heaven or hell?*

"Don't stall me too long, Danny. I don't want the administration to think I'm a dissident. I love my life here with you and the Youth Council." Lydia changed the subject. "Tomorrow, Omega I is supposed to make an important announcement. Do you think he'll announce the winners of the contest for initiatives?"

Daniel didn't know what announcement the president intended to make. He was overwhelmed with thinking about the future or whether he and Lydia would even have one. From his perspective, the future grew dimmer and dimmer. "I don't know; guess we'll hear tomorrow."

Omega I and the Prophet watched the Youth Council file in and take their seats. Daniel noted that the Prophet who usually ran the Council meetings had a dark and sinister look today. He sensed that many of the new initiatives began in the Prophet's mind. An oppressing aura of evil filled the Council chamber as Omega I began to speak.

"My dear children, in exactly one week the City of Gold will be revealed to the world via satellite. As Youth Council members, you will have an honored role to play. At this unveiling, you will be asked to show your complete trust and loyalty to me and to the new system. A wreath of victory will be placed on the head of the winner of the travel to anywhere in the world and he or she will be inaugurated as the president of the Youth Council.

"At this point, I'll let my colleague Vice President Prophet take over the meeting." The president shook hands in greeting then added, "Justin is my eyes and ears, my friend and ally. And as most of you know, he is responsible for bringing me back to life after the assassination attempt last year. Justin." A low murmur resonated through the Council.

A huge burst of applause greeted the Prophet. The dark and sinister look left his face and he seemed to glow with energy not of this world. Intense loathing and repulsion swept over Daniel. *Why did he feel this way?*

As if the Prophet discerned even one who was not in tune, his eyes singled out Daniel. "The president and I chose you to be the seeds of a new world order. Your lives are blessed with riches and good living. In one week, you will be asked to show the world your loyalty and love for Omega I and this new world. Remember, your future depends on your absolute obedience and trust. You will be instructed before the broadcast. Let there be no hesitation in your response."

The meeting adjourned. Lydia and Daniel left together. Daniel was somber.

"What do you think they'll ask us to do?"

"I have no idea."

"You're upset, Danny?"

"I want to succeed in the Youth Council."

"But..."

"But, I get terrible vibes when I'm around the Prophet and the statue. Ever since I was at the retraining center and took those drugs, I sense evil and darkness. The Prophet and the statue both set off those alarms."

Lydia didn't know how to comfort Daniel. She didn't feel any danger or darkness. She loved her life in the City of Gold. It was magic. She wished she knew how to help Daniel. They reached her apartment, and Daniel kissed her goodnight. "Coming in?"

"Not tonight. I need some alone time."

Daniel unlocked his suite and turned on the media center. If he didn't lighten up, he was afraid he'd lose Lydia. He stretched out in his leather recliner to watch the news. The weather channel's coverage could keep you glued day and night. In the spring, the Midwest experienced tornadoes and floods. The South drought, in the West forest fires burned hundreds of acres of forest land. In Arizona and Texas merciless heat defied all known records since the 1800s. Mother

Nature was definitely sending out a warning. Even earthquakes occurred in unexpected states like Virginia, with ricocheting waves felt as far away as Michigan. If nature reflected God, He was certainly upset.

Chapter Eleven

The Youth Council met daily working diligently on their education initiatives. Some of the education proposals the Council of Twelve passed disappointed Daniel. Upset that the Council was substituting a course in high school on the initiatives to replace U.S. history, Daniel discussed the decision with Lydia.

"Don't you think it's important that kids realize that Americans gave up their lives in many wars to fight for our freedoms?"

"I don't think it's as important as knowing the history and thinking behind each initiative," said Lydia. "The past is gone, Daniel. It's a new century with wonderful possibilities. We need to look ahead not behind. For example, if they can understand why older people aren't given costly, life-saving surgeries when they are near the end of their lives, they'll accept the Ascension and other health initiatives better."

Daniel stared at her. "How can you support the gassing of older citizens who've fought in wars, paid their taxes, and been good citizens?"

"Danny, I feel sad about your grandparents but there's a bigger purpose here—the good of the many. Think how the money saved helps the economy. If America goes bankrupt we all lose."

Daniel shook his head and spoke quietly, "Our forefathers cared about individuals, individual freedoms to health and happiness. One person meant a lot."

"I think that's a selfish point of view, Danny. We need to think about what helps the most people. I'm sorry, but we can't just think of what's good for us personally. Smart people, thoughtful, educated people work out these initiatives."

"What about the one the Council of Twelve passed today?" Daniel asked. "What do you think of personality profiling?"

"I think it's really exciting. I want to do a video following a person as they are profiled, counseled and choose their career path and subjects. I really think this will help kids fulfill their destinies better."

"You don't see anything wrong with tracking them at an early age to a career? China's been doing that forever."

"And look where it's gotten them...they are the world leader in manufacturing. Their education standards produce more mathematicians and engineers than we ever have."

"You don't see any danger in this? What if the country needed bricklayers or TV repairmen and your dream was to go to college to be a professor like your parents but you tested high in technical dexterity. Would you be happy to give up your dream?"

Lydia shook her head. "I don't know, Danny. Do you really think they'd track people into careers they didn't want?"

"Yes."

"What about our Constitution? Do you think we should let a document written in the 1700s be our guide for today?"

"You don't?"

"No, I think all you have to do is look at this dynamic city to know we are entering a new era and need a new constitution."

Daniel left Lydia and walked back to his condo, disappointed that Lydia bought the administration's line. The Youth Council was being very subtly brainwashed to mold their support for all the hateful initiatives the administration dreamed up. Was he the only one on the Youth Council who saw the danger?

In the days to come Daniel saw less and less of Lydia who spent endless hours perfecting and shooting her promotion for use in high schools when they returned to their home states as ambassadors. Daniel was thankful his plan to hire personal trainers for high school was popular with the Youth Council. Even the Prophet was impressed at the impact on future health costs. Needing to work off some anger and frustration, Daniel headed to the racketball courts. He'd see Lydia later for dinner, if she had time.

The following week, the Council tackled what to do with world history classes, voting to replace them with a course called "The Global Community." The content for the new course included chapters on the World Federation (global politics and treaties), One World Finances, the new financial system uniting the world with the taking of the number, and the One World Religion with a historical look at religion as the cause of wars. It included footage from the recent closing of Bible-based churches in America.

Each change in the curriculum eroded and erased the rights guaranteed by the Constitution.

Daniel struggled with the idea that this government would either propel America into a wonderful new age of change or convert America into a godless cog in the global wheel of government.

President Blackstone looked out over his glittering, futuristic city. No city in this world compared to its beauty. He felt like god. And his creation **was** good. He turned to the Prophet who'd entered his office. "Is everything ready?"

"The calla lilies and orchids arrived this morning from California, a gift of the governor and are being planted as we speak." The Prophet joined Omega I in surveying the beautiful city. "The people of America should be pleased with their new capital."

At first the Board of Governors violently resisted moving the capital out of Washington D.C. But after a tour of the city and a view of the luxurious suites and facilities, all objections to moving the capital vanished. The chemical engineers at Sky Dome Enterprises created a dome even nuclear weapons could not penetrate.

The president hated for the world to discover the location of the new city. People entered the city by invitation only and, in truth, that was the way the president liked it. But the unveiling of the City of Gold was set for three p.m.

Chapter Twelve

L ydia finished putting on her makeup. A knock on the door of her suite sent her rushing to open it, hoping to find Daniel. A Guardian handed her an envelope embossed with gold. She opened the envelope to find an announcement that she had won the contest for initiatives with her national promotion. She would receive the wreath of victory, and would be named president of the Youth Council. She closed the door and sat down, tears running down her cheeks. She never thought they would make a girl president of the Council. Should she tell Daniel when he came to pick her up or let him be surprised? Daniel was her friend. She needed to spend more time with him and she hoped he was proud of her achievements.

Daniel showered and dressed in the Council's sapphire robe. He wished he could see his family and friends' reactions to the City of Gold. He had to admit, the city was unlike any place he'd ever seen. And despite some of the choices the Youth Council made, Daniel was still proud to be a member. The Prophet informed the members that their parents had received a letter about the media tour and formal induction of the Council. All eyes would be on the City of Gold at three p.m.

He picked up Lydia at her suite and they walked slowly to the Council chambers which opened onto the beautiful gardens surrounding the golden statue. Hundreds of state flowers surrounded the statue: white flowering dogwoods from North Carolina, pink peonies from Indiana, magnolias from Louisiana, orange California poppies, and sunflowers from Kansas as well as all the other state flowers.

"Oh Danny, look the states have all sent their state flowers. How wonderful!"

Daniel didn't answer, wondering who would be named president of the Youth Council and receive the victory wreath. And the other question that haunted him was, would this induction require something else from the Council?

Before the presentation, the Prophet took the podium and instructed the young people: "Remember who you are—the chosen of Omega I. You are America's hope for the future, privileged to be counted as Omega I's children. All he demands is your loyalty and honor. At the proper time, you will be asked to show that loyalty and will be told what to say and do. Remember, the world is watching."

A lump rose in Lydia's throat. The whole world, her parents, Daniel's parents would see her receive the wreath of victory. She tried to focus on the instructions they were being given.

Daniel feared the worst. *Why was the Prophet being so secretive?*

Noticing the cloud on Daniel's face, Lydia took his hand. "Everything will be fine, you'll see."

At three p.m. the government preempted all television channels to broadcast the viewing of the City of Gold. Omega I stepped in front of the cameras, his voice soft and seductive, drawing in each viewer on a personal tour through his beautiful new city. The transition was skillfully made from the familiar Washington, D.C. scene showing its graveyards and memorials to the unearthly beauty of the blue-glass city with its streets of translucent gold and its fountains and gardens—the contrast shocking. Finally, the cameras rested on the faces of the Youth Council dressed in their sapphire robes. "Now I would like to present to the nation the President's Youth Council, the young people who will have an important role in our government."

"Momma, there's Danny. That must be Lydia next to him. She's so beautiful," Penny said.

Judith sat enraptured, tears running down her cheeks. It was her moment as well as Daniel's. Omega I had said "young people who will have a role in our government"— her son, Daniel. She looked at Harry. Deep worry lines carved his face. *Where was his joy? His pride?*

Penny moved closer to her mother, squeezing her hand while they watched.

The camera shifted from Omega I to the golden statue— its likeness to the president eerie. And then as if an afterthought, the president turned and signaled the Prophet to take over.

"Here before us are the young people who, as the president told you, we are training to rule. They are America's future. They will be given much. Only one thing will be asked of them—complete loyalty."

As the Prophet finished, the amazing statue appeared to come to life, speaking directly to the Youth Council. "Come children, bow before me. Fall on your knees and repeat these words: You are the Alpha and Omega. We give you our lives." Smoke rolled from the image as it spoke. Its eyes penetrated the Youth Council lined up two by two before it.

In that moment Daniel realized they were being asked for the unquestioning loyalty he'd seen in the faces of Hitler's SS Corps in films his world history class viewed in high school. *How could he get near the golden statue when it had called him a doubter?* Whatever or whoever programmed this technical wonder—it was the enemy. Daniel could not pledge allegiance, much less his life before it. Each pair of Youth Council members, seduced by the moment, walked to the foot of the statue, fell on their knees, and repeated the words, "We give you our lives."

Beads of perspiration broke out on Daniel's forehead. An inner pounding stirred his heart. He could not...would not... bow before the golden statue. It represented evil to Daniel. Trying to think, he took Lydia's hand and let the other Youth Council members go around him. *What should he do? What would it cost him if he refused to bow before the statue? Would it cost him his friendship with Lydia?*

Unlike Lydia, Daniel had seen destruction and death as a result of Omega I and the Prophet—Bibles burned, churches closed, and the death of many innocents at the Ascensions.

No matter what it cost him, Daniel could not bow down and say those words. Lydia tugged on Daniel's sleeve. "I can't, Lydia," he whispered. "It's wrong. I don't know why; I just know."

The last two Youth Council members moved down the aisle toward the idol. The victory wreath had not yet been presented. "Go ahead, Lydia. I can't do it."

Lydia's hands were shaking. *Not now, Daniel. Don't leave now. I'm going to be inducted as the president of the Youth Council. I'm to receive the victory wreath. Where are you going? Do you know what you are doing? Please don't ruin our future.* But Daniel walked away, head down, leaving Lydia with the greatest decision of her life. Should she let him go?

Chapter Thirteen

Lydia watched Daniel walk away, desperate to know what to do. She watched as two of the Prophet's men grabbed him. One of them shoved Daniel to the ground, placing his foot on Daniel's back while signaling the other man to shackle him.

Lydia stood paralyzed. *Why were they hurting Daniel?* She wanted to scream. This was the City of Gold. Daniel hadn't done anything. Forgetting for the moment that she was to receive the victory wreath, Lydia ran to catch up with Daniel. "Wait, what are you doing? He's not a criminal. Let him go." Daniel's head hit the pavement. Lydia saw blood running down his face into his eyes.

"Go back, Lydia. Go back while there's still time."

Lydia stood frozen. Then, suddenly, one of the guards grabbed her and pushed her forward behind Daniel. Her hesitation to return to the line to bow before the statue now cost her whatever future she would have had in the Youth Council.

"Let me go. You can't treat us like this."

The men ignored her, dragging both her and Daniel out of the view of the cameras. The guards had been instructed by the Prophet in the event a Youth Council member did not bow before the golden statue, they were to be taken to his office. He would deal with them personally.

They pushed Daniel and Lydia into the waiting room. Daniel saw terror reflected in Lydia's eyes. *What could he say? What had his refusal to bow before the statue cost them?* He knew there would be no mercy. You didn't cross the Prophet.

They waited an hour. Finally, the Prophet called them into his office. Reluctantly, Lydia and Daniel entered the room and stood before him.

"So…you two decided you would not bow before Omega I's statue."

Lydia responded, "No, Prophet. I followed Daniel because your men were hurting him, not because I couldn't bow before the statue." Lydia was shaking. Daniel said nothing.

The Prophet ignored her. Turning to Daniel he said, "One purpose of the golden image is to sift out unbelievers. You are Daniel Jordan, are you not?"

"Yes, I am."

"What do you have to say for yourself, Daniel?"

"I have nothing to say, Prophet."

"I am surprised at you, Lydia. Did you tell Daniel that you won the wreath of victory, were to be president of the Youth Council and receive the vacation to anywhere in the world?"

The color drained from Lydia's face. Startled, Daniel realized what Lydia was giving up in her concern for his safety. "Lydia, go back. This is my decision. It doesn't have to be yours."

The Prophet waited for Lydia to answer. In truth their lives were whatever the Prophet and Omega I wished. They belonged to him whether they bowed before the idol or not.

Daniel looked at Lydia. "I didn't know; I'm so sorry."

What should she do? Her life in the City of Gold was like a fairy tale. She'd met so many new friends including Daniel. Her wildest dreams had become a reality with winning the victor's wreath and being named president of the Youth Council. And yet, in this one horrendous moment, she saw the brutality of the Prophet. She'd bought into the whole program. Possibly, Daniel's suspicions were right. Lydia dropped her head, ashamed that she'd disregarded Daniel's warnings. "I told you, I followed Daniel because he's my friend and your men were hurting him. Neither of us have done anything wrong."

The Prophet turned his back on the two Youth Council members. He'd hoped for 100 percent obedience to the oath of loyalty. And these two...two of the most promising members... disappointed him. Tired of waiting on Lydia's answer, the Prophet addressed the two guards. "Take them to their rooms. I'll deal with them later."

The Prophet ran the footage of the initiation, pleased the cameras hadn't picked up Daniel and Lydia. To the world, the Youth Council showed total allegiance and worshipped Omega I's statue. Unknown to the Youth Council, each person bowing before the golden statue now belonged to Omega I. An evil smile played across the Prophet's face. The idol had done its first weeding out of the unfaithful—those who did not belong.

It was over. Would they be sent home or somewhere else to finish their duty? Although Daniel didn't know about Lydia's success, he made the only decision he could make. Sooner or later, he and the administration with all their terrible initiatives would part. He wouldn't have taken the number. But Lydia...had given up her whole world. Overwhelmed with fear, Daniel dreaded the future. *Where would the Prophet send them?*

Tears rolled down Lydia's cheeks turning into torrents of sobs. *What had she done? Had she made a mistake?* She could be reinstated, but she didn't know if she wanted to be part of an evil administration who demanded complete loyalty but didn't care about individuals. *What should she do? And why hadn't Daniel been able to bow before the statue?* She sank down on her bed, her heart breaking with all she'd lost. *Would she be sent home?*

In the morning the MPs escorted Daniel and Lydia to a military van. No one spoke to them and they had no idea where they were being taken. They rode in silence. Lydia squeezed Daniel's hand until he could no longer feel anything.

She must be very frightened, he thought.

Daniel's parents stared at the satellite screen. Judith was frantic. "Where was Daniel, Harry? Where was he? Did you see the girl he called Lydia?"

"No, I didn't see either of them."

"What could have happened? I'm going to call the City of Gold."

Harry frowned. "No, Judith, you aren't."

Judith had never heard Harry use that tone of voice.

"If you don't want to endanger yourself, Penny, and me, then stay off the phone. Daniel is enough."

"What do you mean? What do you mean Daniel is enough?"

"I think Daniel believes in the old ways. He got it from Pa. He couldn't bow before a statue. It's that simple."

"It isn't simple to me," Judith screamed. "What are you saying? Daniel gave up his whole future because of some weird teachings from your father?"

"Judith, Daniel made his decision. His friend must have decided to stay with him."

"How could he do this to us?" raged Judith. "Why couldn't he obey his authorities? What did they ever do to Daniel except give him the most wonderful life?" Judith broke down in sobs.

Penny had been very quiet. They'd forgotten she was in the room with them. "Daddy, will they hurt Daniel?"

"I don't know, Pen. I don't know." But Harry knew Daniel had made his choice. He believed in his son. *May the God of heaven watch over you, Daniel. You are in His hands now.*

Chapter Fourteen

O mega I was disappointed to lose two Youth Council members in the test of loyalty, especially two such promising young people, but that was one of its purposes — to filter out the unfaithful. The chosen ones must be believers in the new regime.

The president leaned back in his chair. *What if the parents of the two Youth Council members contacted legal services or the media?* Perhaps he needed to draft a formal communication not to interfere or pursue their whereabouts. He could sound disappointed and say, "I am saddened at their loss." All true.

He picked up Daniel and Lydia's files and thrust them into the shredder then sent a memo to contact California and Arizona to make another selection. Omega I suspected the

Prophet had already arranged for their removal from the City of Gold.

The van headed north. *Where were they taking them? Were they being sent home?*

Daniel thought about his life since high school—a rough ride. A sharp pain stabbed his brain. He still experienced residual effects from the laser treatments. Surely, they weren't taking them to a retraining center. Sweat beaded on his forehead dripping into his eyes, but he didn't loosen his hand from Lydia's. A feeling of hopelessness gnawed at him. Lydia stared out her window. He shouldn't have allowed her to stay with him. She had no idea of the brutality of this regime. He put his arm around her drawing her close. "I'm sorry, Lydia, so sorry." He squeezed her hand and she looked into his eyes. He saw fear. *With so much at stake, why hadn't Lydia returned to receive the wreath of victory? Did the guards' violence surprise her, causing her to doubt?*

A brick fortress appeared out of the fog, its iron gates forbidding. A real prison? The van stopped. The driver showed his identification and the iron gates swung open, clanging shut behind them. Scared to death, Lydia gripped Daniel's hand; tears raced down her cheeks. "Danny, I thought they'd send us home. Is this a real prison?"

Daniel nodded. He wondered what kind of criminals the prison held. Roughly, the guards pulled them out of the van. "Where are we?" Daniel asked. "Is this a dissident prison?"

"You could say that. We got more types in here than a zoo."

The young couple followed the guards into a large gray room with heavy metal bars on the windows. The pock-marked concrete floor bore little of its original paint. Light bulbs hung from the ceiling casting dark shadows on the walls and floor. The two sat down on cheap metal chairs to wait.

Fear broke loose in Lydia like a thunderstorm releasing its fury and sweeping every normal feeling away. In one decision, her perfect life crumbled. She'd lost everything— her future, the City of Gold, and her family. Afraid to talk, Lydia shot glances at Daniel.

Soon an old woman with steel eyes and dingy gray hair signaled Lydia to follow her. Lydia turned to Daniel. "Danny..."

"He can't help you here. Follow me."

Lydia followed the harsh old woman into a locker room.

"Take off your clothes." The matron pointed to the showers, handing Lydia a primitive cake of soap and towel. Icy water stung her skin and the soap left red marks wherever she washed. The matron watched as Lydia washed with the coarse soap.

"Hair, too," she rasped.

Lydia stared at the soap—a symbol of her lost world. She rinsed her hair in the cold water, shivering uncontrollably. She finished toweling dry and looked up to see the woman holding a huge pair of scissors in her hand. The woman shoved her down on a stone bench and began to chop off Lydia's beautiful hair. She sheared her like a sheep. No emotion, no words.

For the first time, Lydia understood what her decision cost. The tears that wouldn't come now flooded her cheeks. When the matron finished, she threw washed-out blue scrubs at Lydia.

"Put these on and follow me."

Lydia did as she was told. She was no longer Lydia Cohen. Her hope lay on the floor mixed with the lost chestnut hair.

The Cohens sat on the porch of their San Diego home, enjoying the view of the coastline.

"Open the letter, Samuel," Lydia's mother said.

Samuel took a letter opener and carefully cut along the edge. He lifted out the formal letter from the president and read it out loud.

Lydia's mother's face registered her concern. "I was hoping Lydia wouldn't get trapped in this government's web. I think she'd have taken the number. She said as much when she was here. What do you think happened, Samuel?"

"I don't know." Samuel folded the letter and replaced it in its envelope. There was no further discussion.

Trained under the harsh discipline of the Guardians, Daniel sat stone-like while the guard shaved his head, a gesture meant to humiliate and intimidate him. Daniel's resolve hardened. He wasn't easy to intimidate and he could hold his own with any Guardian on duty. The problem was they were armed and he wasn't and this prison was a fortress.

He thought about Lydia, sure his lovely friend had never experienced anything but kindness. How would she survive? His stubborn sense of right and wrong had brought him and Lydia to a dreadful state. *What had they done to his lovely and faithful friend? How could he ever look her in the eyes again? Oh God, what have I done?"*

"What's the name of this prison?" Daniel asked.

The guard laughed. "What difference does it make?"

Daniel knew they were still in Kansas. They'd only driven an hour. He tried to remember what prisons were in Kansas and suddenly it came to him. They were in Leavenworth, an old military prison the administration must have taken over.

"Don't worry, buddy. There's a lot going on here. They'll probably put you on some labor crew. We need lots of labor—you know garbage crew, latrine cleaning crew, or maybe they'll put you on some special project. Leavenworth is one of the Prophet's projects, ya know."

Daniel could just imagine. Get rid of any objectors to the system. He peered into the cells as the Guardian led him to a small filthy room with two striped cots.

"If you're cooperative, you may get a roommate someday. Someone to share your bed, complain to, have in-depth conversations with, someone to arm wrestle."

Daniel wished this clown would shut up. The gate slid open and the Guardian deposited Daniel. "No chow till morning. But you look pretty well fed."

Daniel couldn't stop thinking about Lydia. *Would she survive this hostile environment? Would he?* He couldn't bear to think about it. He buried his head in his hands. The pain was back, stabbing his mind and his heart. *"I couldn't make it Captain. I tried but I couldn't make it. You were right. Something else is wrong...I think your president and the Prophet are the most evil men I've ever met."*

Harry left the stables early. He checked the mail, usually Judith's job, but she'd taken Penny shopping. Leafing through the envelopes, he discovered a legal-looking document from the government.

Holding his breath, he ripped the letter open hoping, for some word of Daniel's fate. The signature had the stamp of the president. He read:

"On May 5, 2024, Daniel Jordan and Lydia Cohen submitted their resignations from the Youth Council. They were immediately transferred to a government facility to finish their commitment. No contact is advised at this time. You will be notified of their progress in the future. We are disappointed to lose their service in the Youth Council but in a free nation, the individual has choice."

One Nation of the Globe Under Omega I

What did this letter mean? What government facility did they transfer them to? So Harry was right...no further contact advised...a warning.

Chapter Fifteen

Pain seared through nurse Nan Coleman's heart when she thought of her old boss, Dr. Hart. Why would his former college friend, the president, have a car bomb planted to eliminate him?

She loved the work at Rancho Christo taking care of the patients Dr. Hart transferred from their clinic in Phoenix but lately, a nagging worry tugged at her. What happened to Daniel Jordan, the Guardian who drove the patients to Rancho Christo? If the government coerced information from Daniel while he was at Fort Thompson—the mind retraining center—the ranch could be in danger. She had to know. She voice dialed her pastor, Neal Matthews, now living in her Scottsdale apartment.

"Please be home, pastor," she whispered.

The phone rang six times, then a male voice asked, "Yes, who is it?"

"Pastor, it's me, Nan; I'm calling from the ranch."

Relieved Neal switched the phone to his right hand. Since he'd become a dissident pastor losing his church to the One World religion, he was on edge every time the phone rang. "Go ahead, Nan."

"Do you remember me mentioning the young Guardian, Daniel Jordan?"

"Vaguely, he drove…"

"Right…patients here. I can't get him off my heart. And I can't shake the feeling that we need to find him. He's the only who could compromise our safe house."

Pastor Neal scratched his head. ""Do you know where his parents live?"

"I know they run a guest ranch. I think Daniel said it was by the Verde River."

"I'll see what I can do, Nan. We miss you."

"Pastor, don't stay in Phoenix too long. We need you here at Rancho Christo. I'll keep in touch by email. Let me know what you find out."

Pastor Neal pushed the red button on his digital phone. It was nine p.m. He turned on his computer pulling up the

Scottsdale directory. Ninety-nine Jordans, but only twenty-seven in Scottsdale. He ruled out all but four—E. Princess, E. Sahuaro, E. La Hunta, and one on Trails End. It might be dangerous to call Daniel's home if the government had him in some kind of prison. Pastor Neal suspected the government monitored phone lines on dissidents...but he trusted God. If He was issuing the order, Neal would be protected. He prayed and decided to begin with the possibility that a guest ranch might be located on Trails End.

"Jordan residence," a male voice answered.

"Is this Daniel Jordan's father?"

The line grew quiet. Harry Jordan took a deep breath. *Was this man a friend or enemy? Was this a trick to see if Daniel had come home?*

"Mr. Jordan, my name is Pastor Neal Matthews. Dr. Hart's nurse asked me to call and ask about Daniel. She was fond of him."

"Pastor, I don't know where Daniel is."

Neal detected sadness and anger in Mr. Jordan's voice. "I know this is unusual but...would you come to my apartment for coffee...say, in the morning early?"

Harry hesitated. "I'm sorry. I need to be on the range very early."

"Would five a.m. work for you?"

"If you insist." Harry wrote down directions. The truth was he was sick with worry about Daniel. His son's whereabouts were constantly on his mind. *Where are you, Daniel? What have they done with you?* Perhaps it would be good to talk to someone other than Judith.

In the morning Harry left a note saying he was meeting a friend for coffee. Judith slept in till at least eight a.m. He drove to the apartment on Mountain View thinking it odd that a minister lived in an apartment. He rang the doorbell and a clean-shaven man with light, graying hair opened the door. His smile put Harry at ease.

"Come in. Harry Jordan, isn't it?"

"Yes, sir, thank you."

Pastor Neal walked into the kitchenette and poured Harry a steaming mug of coffee while beckoning him into a small great room. They sat quietly for a minute.

"I know you must think it odd—my call," Pastor Neal began, "but Dr. Hart's nurse asked…"

"He was killed in a car bomb accident?"

Neal looked up. "Probably not an accident. Nan feels the administration knew he resisted the initiatives of the president. He'd designed the Center for New Age Medicine but it took a different direction from the one he'd envisioned."

"The Ascension?"

"Yes, and other programs. But let's talk about Daniel. You knew he drove patients to a safe house for the doctor?"

Harry's surprise was visible. "No, I didn't. Did Daniel know he was transporting people out of the system?"

"I don't know the answer to that...he may have...or not. I think that's part of Nan's concern about Daniel. This must all be very upsetting to you, Mr. Jordan."

Harry looked down. "My wife has disowned Daniel. She acts like she never had a son."

"Have you taken the number?"

"No, I haven't...don't intend to...that's another thing that upsets her. She's a very angry woman now. And...I'm a very lonely man. I miss my son."

"Why don't you tell me about Daniel after he was picked up by the military police."

Harry didn't know what to say. The pastor seemed kind and concerned so he told him what little they knew.

"Do you think they did mind retraining on Daniel?"

"Yes, but he wouldn't talk about it."

"Mr. Jordan, I don't know how to ask this, but if Daniel knew something that could incriminate someone, would he reveal it to the authorities?"

"Daniel is a caring person. That's why his work for Dr. Hart upset him. He hated the Ascension and felt like he was betraying the old people assigned to it. His grandparents were in the 1st Ascension—he never got over their death. He told me he felt like he should be protecting the old and sick, not helping the government destroy them. I'm sorry, I've said too much. But to answer your question, I don't believe Daniel would reveal anything if he thought he would endanger someone. He's very loyal."

"When was the last time you saw him?"

"He was home on spring break…couldn't say enough about the City of Gold and all the president was doing for them. He even met a beautiful girl there. The Youth Council was working on some new education initiatives. My wife and I thought he was very happy."

"So he became a Youth Council member?"

"The captain at the retraining center liked Daniel. I suppose he wanted to give him a new start. He sent him to the City of Gold to serve on the president's Youth Council."

The pastor watched Harry carefully, seeing his eyes cloud up. "What happened?"

"I knew he was in for trouble because he wasn't going to take the mark to buy and sell. Everything was furnished for the Council members so he hadn't had to take it. But he couldn't be so high in government without taking it. Something you should understand, Daniel's grandparents came to live with us for about six months before the Ascension occurred. My dad gave Daniel his Bible and he read a lot about what was coming in the future."

"He wasn't able to bow before the golden statue, was he?"

"No, evidently not. We never saw him...his name wasn't announced and neither was his friend Lydia's. We received a threatening letter warning us not to try to locate him." Embarrassed, Harry used his sleeve to wipe away the tears streaming down his weathered face. "We have no idea what they've done with them."

Pastor Neal sat quietly. "I'm sorry, Mr. Jordan. I lost my church to this new administration and now I'm a dissident myself. I can't take the number so I've lost my home and here I am in Nan's apartment with only a few weeks left before I leave here."

"Where will you go?"

"I'll go to one of the safe houses. Do you know about them?"

"No. Places for people who can't take the number?"

"Something like that. There's a large underground net-work—ranches and farms growing their own food, digging wells, essentially becoming pioneers."

"Would there be one near the City of Gold?"

"I'm not sure. Let's look on my map and see. We have an underground network on the computer also." With that he brought up a map and Harry leaned over his shoulder to see better. "Liberty Farm is the only one close by. It's east of the City of Gold. Why do you ask?"

"Could you contact them and ask them to be on the lookout for Daniel and his friend?"

A sudden pounding started in Neal's chest, one he'd learned to know as the Holy Spirit wanting to get his attention. Did God want this man to contact Liberty Farm? His heartbeat grew stronger. *Okay, Lord, I'll help him.* Neal saw the intensity in Harry's eyes. The good father needed to do something to help his son. "A good idea, Harry. I'll give you the address and email Liberty to watch for your son and his friend."

Harry shook hands with the pastor, an idea forming in his mind. He took the address and hurried to his SUV. There was one thing he could do.

Chapter Sixteen

Harry had a plan, but he wasn't sure how to approach Judith. He didn't want her to know where he was going. He drove home by reflex, unaware what streets he crossed. Entering the house he heard the shower. He pushed the kitchen butler producing a couple of hot mugs of coffee and sat down to wait for his wife.

"Harry, I thought you'd be out on the range."

He pushed the coffee toward her. "No, I wanted to talk with you before I go out. I need to spend a week checking on the herd. I'll drive my truck but I'd like a gas card in case of emergencies—several hundred dollars. Do you have time to purchase it for me?"

"Will three hundred be enough?"

Harry bluffed, "Let's make it for five hundred, then I won't have to bother you so often." Harry hesitated, a thought occurring to him. "I'd like it in two cards of two fifty each. Will you be all right while I'm gone?"

Judith shook her head. She really didn't care what Harry did anymore. "Go ahead, Harry. We'll be fine."

"I'm going to give the motorcycle away. I've asked Joey to come over."

Judith continued to sip her coffee. She didn't care what Harry did with the motorcycle as long as it was out of her sight. She wanted no reminders of Daniel. He was gone... out of their lives...hard to believe her favorite betrayed her. She'd waste no more time thinking about Daniel. Perhaps while Harry was gone, she'd clean out Daniel's room. She agreed that Joey could use the motorcycle. His old jalopy was near death.

"Fine, Harry, do what you want with it. I don't need it around here to remind me of...of the past."

Harry hated the role of deceiver. He'd always been honest and up front with Judith but things were different now. His primary concern was helping Daniel. He filled the two gas tanks in the truck from their ranch pump. Daniel had filled the Black Mustang on spring break but Harry needed to charge the cycle's alternative hybrid motor overnight.

He cleaned the truck windows with Rainex and checked the gauges, making sure the tire pressure was correct. The truck was ready. After lunch he rode out to the northeast fence that needed repair and then up to the caves. If Daniel intended to be a Christian, he would need Grandpa's box with the Bible.

Next Harry pulled up the pantry contents on the kitchen butler, relieved to see a number of camping provisions. He pushed the numbers to choose a case of water, beans, a bag of apples, trail mix, and salami, placing them in the space behind the front seats. *Had he thought of everything?* He heard the door bang. Penny must be home.

"Hi, Dad, Mom says you're leaving for a few days. She told me to give you these gas cards." Penny paused. "Are you going to try to find Danny, Dad?"

Startled by Penny's intuition, Harry braced himself. The less Penny knew, the safer she'd be. He hated to lie to her but, "No, Pen, just checking on the herds. I may give them some antibiotics while I'm up there. Joey's bringing over a supply."

Penny put her arms around her dad. "If you see Danny, tell him I love him."

Harry felt sad that after twenty-five years of marriage, he could count on Penny more than his wife. If Judith discovered his real purpose for this trip, it would be brutal. "Thanks, Pen, take care of your mom."

Harry looked down at his daughter. If Daniel was right, Penny would be asked to go on the Lamb's project next year. He'd do everything he could to protect her even if it meant the end of his marriage. Judith loved the new system and would no doubt see the Lamb's project as some kind of honor for Penny. As far as Harry was concerned the new government had presented nothing but problems. First Grandpa and Jenny, then Daniel, next...*one crisis at a time,* he thought.

Trying to relax before his trip, Harry took out a beer and settled into his recliner to watch the eleven o'clock news. Realizing he must have dozed off, he snapped awake as he heard the newscaster introduce Omega I. What was President Blackstone saying?

"For twenty years, a shortage of organ donors has existed. After much consideration and study, we have come up with a new solution. All lifers and those sentenced to death will be given the opportunity to do a final good act for society. There is no greater love than to give one's life for another. Inmates can choose to end their life in honor.

"They will be humanely put to sleep and their organs harvested to give someone new life. Those who choose to end their life in this way will be given a state funeral and all their criminal records erased. The families of these prisoners will no longer feel disgrace."

Harry tried to digest this newest initiative. Was Daniel in prison? Was this some new way to get rid of those who opposed the government? *My God...Daniel.* He turned off the news. His body felt like lead. *Daniel, son, where are you?*

Harry slept like a man in a coma. He awakened and for a moment didn't know where he was. Five a.m. As he dressed, he thought about what he'd tell the people at Liberty Farm— Daniel's story. He'd leave the motorcycle with them asking that they give it to Daniel if he showed up. *Did his plan make sense? It* was the best he could do. "*Oh, God, if you really can hear, watch over my son,*" he whispered.

At five-thirty a.m. he met Joey at the barn. "Thanks for bringing over the antibiotics, Joey."

"No problem, Mr. J. Can I help you load the Honda? Are you taking it to Daniel?"

"Not exactly. I'm giving it to some people who need it."

"I miss Daniel; he was a good friend. You could count on him, you know?"

"I know, Joey. Can I drop you somewhere?"

"Not necessary, sir. I've still got my old jalopy. She's purring like a kitten."

"Take care, you'll make a great vet and thank Doc for the antibiotics. I'll do a little preventative care. Don't want my beef infected." He watched Joey climb into his old auto. Sports had protected both Joey and Daniel, keeping them busy and out of trouble. *Why, oh why, didn't Daniel go to the College of Professional Athletes?* The answer was simple. Judith, of course. Daniel tried to please his politically-motivated mother. Harry was no less guilty. *Why hadn't he supported Daniel's desire to play professional soccer?* Deciding not to wake Judith, Harry left a note on the kitchen bar, cocked his Stetson, and took a deep breath. "Well, let's have a little adventure," he said to himself.

The longest stretch he'd driven was seventeen hours, but he liked driving at night, so he'd drive as long as he could. If he got too tired, he'd pull into a campground and sleep. He leaned over and programmed the GPS for the Kansas farm. Highway 87 through Payson to Highway 40 avoided Flagstaff and the highly-policed Highway 17.

Traffic was light, and following the serpentine path of the mountain highway calmed Harry. He was amazed that man bulldozed and blasted a super highway through the deep gorges in the Mogollon mountain range.

Hair-trigger cameras monitored all highways and since Harry hadn't taken the number, he couldn't afford to get pulled over by the police. He glanced in the rearview mirror to see if the Honda was riding all right. As he neared Gallup, he noticed a sheriff's car pull in back of him. Harry wiped sweat from his brow. Was the sheriff's car following him or was it on a routine run? A flashing red light answered his question. He pulled off the highway as soon as it was safe and stayed in the truck.

A Native American officer dressed in a brown uniform with pants riding the top of his socks and serious sunglasses came to the driver's side. Harry held his breath.

"Sir, roll down your window."

"Something wrong, officer?"

"You aware you got something sparking under your truck?"

"No, sir, can I check it out?" Harry opened the car door and slid under the truck. A loose muffler was dragging the pavement. "Muffler," he yelled.

"Need some wire?"

"Thanks, that'd help."

The officer opened his trunk and cut off a length of heavy duty wire taking a length to Harry. "Try this."

Harry grabbed the wire, anchored the muffler, then crawled out from under the truck. He relaxed, trying not to look like he'd robbed a bank.

"Yep, happens every now and then. My motto's be prepared."

"A good motto. Is it all right for me to go now?"

"Gotta nice motorcycle back here."

Harry began to sweat again. "Yeah, belongs to my son."

"Used to ride one like this till they put me in the car. Great ride. Yeah, you go on now. Watch that muffler. Get it fixed soon as you can."

"I'll do that. Thanks again."

With relief Harry started the engine and decided to listen to his satellite radio. He especially liked the underground call-in shows that criticized the new government and the president. He wondered how they stayed on the air but assumed they broadcast over a different band each day.

"If you've just joined us, we're discussing the disappearance of some of America's best. If you know someone who's disappeared, give us a call. Today's number is 1-800-Gone. Caller, you're on."

"I'm calling from Chicago. My Aunt Jana disappeared a month ago."

"Was this unexpected?"

"She left her beautiful golden retriever Sienna and a parakeet in her apartment with no food. Sienna's barking upset the other apartment dwellers."

"What do you think happened to your aunt?"

"One old lady in the apartments said she saw two ruffians drag her out without her coat and shove her into a van."

"Tell us about your aunt."

"She was a kind old lady who helped a lot of people."

"Was she a follower of the old ways?"

"I guess. She tried to convince me not to take the number. And I know she was very upset when her church got boarded up."

"She was opposed to the government's new initiatives?"

"Yeah, she held home meetings explaining what the Bible said. She was afraid to go to a doctor for fear they'd put her in the Ascension. It makes me mad. Nice old woman, paid her taxes, lived a kind life. She didn't deserve to be handled like this."

"I'm sorry for your aunt...next caller."

"Oregon."

"Gone in Oregon?"

"Yes sir. My dad's a lawyer. He heads a committee for individual rights."

"That's kind of against the national policy of what's good for the country."

"My dad thought each person was special. He believed in speaking the truth about government policies."

"Deadly. He's gone? Thanks, Oregon."

Harry listened, knowing that his loss was just one of many. Daniel—gone, too.

He hit Albuquerque around two-thirty p.m. surprised at the density of traffic. The overpasses gave the city a modern look. He liked Albuquerque but had visited the city nestled in a valley surrounded by mountains only a few times. Once he'd brought a bus full of ranch tourists up to see the hot air balloon festival. Another time, he'd purchased horses from a private ranch on the north side by Highway 25.

A day later, Harry arrived in Kansas. To the south of Kansas City a large dome rose up like a giant mushroom. He clocked the length—twenty-five miles. Could it be the City of Gold? He checked his location on the GPS, seeing the red dot move toward his target address. Not long now. Pastor Matthews said the farmhouse was on the eastern outskirts of town.

Bill looked up from the water pump. The people of Liberty Farm were never surprised to see strange cars or trucks coming down the road. The farm was self-sufficient. They chopped wood for the fireplace and woodstove, grew and preserved their own crops, burned oil lamps, and fished in the little lake on the property. No one here had taken the number. They couldn't buy or sell. The local people knew their beliefs, but though they didn't share them, they pro-tected their own townsfolk, often dropping off bundles of food and clothing or a little gasoline. The farm was a link in a chain for believers in the old ways.

Bill surveyed the tall, weathered man who climbed out of his truck, judging him to be in his late forties and probably not from around there. His eyes looked tired which meant he'd likely driven straight through from—Bill bent over to see his license plate—Arizona. He welcomed him with a smile, reaching out his hand.

"Bill's the name."

"Harry. Harry Jordan."

"You look tired. How 'bout a cup of coffee?"

Harry smiled. He followed the man into the farmhouse. A huge old-fashioned drip coffeemaker sat on the wood-stove. The scent of apples and spices rose from a kettle next to the coffeepot.

"How did you find us?" Bill asked.

"Pastor Neal Matthews—Scottsdale, Arizona—and a map my father left." Harry took the handmade map out of his jacket pocket."

"How can we help you?"

"Did you get an email last week about a missing young couple? The boy is my son. I'm hoping you can help me."

Bill remembered the strange email. "I did. Tell me about your son."

Harry began the story of Daniel: Daniel—the Guardian; the night of the MPs; the retraining center; the camping trip; the appointment to the Youth Council.

"It sounds like Daniel is a very special young man."

"When they unveiled the City of Gold a few months ago, we—his mother and I—saw him as the cameras panned the Youth Council. But when the names were called, Daniel and his friend Lydia were not among them. That's the last time we saw them. You were the closest safe house to the City of Gold." Harry paused. "Do you have any idea where they would take them?"

Bill knew the administration used the prison at Leavenworth for dissidents. His scouts kept an eye on it, but he didn't want to upset Mr. Jordan. "We have a hunch. We're keeping an eye out for Daniel and his friend. Is there anything else I can do for you, Mr. Jordan?"

"I brought Daniel's Honda motorcycle. I'd like to leave it with you. Please, use it—it's full of gas. Give it to Daniel if you find him. And there is one other favor."

"Shoot."

"My muffler came loose and dragged. Would anyone here be able to see if I'm safe to drive home?"

"Got just the man. I'll have Bert take a look. Let's get you a meal. We'll put you in a bunk after you eat. Looks like you could use a little shut-eye."

"Thanks, I'm beat. I need to get back but I could use a few hours sleep."

Bill smiled and called to his wife. "Honey, you have a customer out here. How 'bout one of those big hearty breakfasts you're so well known for."

Harry relaxed and enjoyed the steaming coffee and the farm breakfast of pancakes, eggs, ham, and fried potatoes. He envied the close relationship he saw between Bill and his wife, Martha, and wished he knew how to reclaim his relationship with Judith.

After Harry and Bill unloaded the cycle, Bill steered Harry to a spare bedroom where he fell asleep with his clothes on. When he awoke, he said goodbye and decided to leave one of the gas cards. He'd done what he could for Daniel. The question was, would Daniel ever find his way to Liberty Farm?

Bill watched Harry drive off. A good father, he thought. He had a hunch about Daniel and the girl. The underground watched the City of Gold closely and noticed helicopters flying between it and the old Leavenworth prison. Bill sus-pected Omega I used Leavenworth for dissidents. The bad news was his scouts had found newly-dug graves. He hoped the young couple was still alive.

Chapter Seventeen

"**M**om, I'm home. Where are you?"

"Back here, Pen, come see."

Penny followed her mother's voice which seemed to be coming from Daniel's room. Gone were Daniel's bed, his soccer poster, and trophies. Instead, Penny saw a mural of Four Peaks mountain range with a stationary bike poised as if to ride off into the desert. Two large cacti surrounded it. In another corner a treadmill faced a wall media center.

"Look, I ordered this water massage table. Isn't it great?"

"But Mom...how could you...it's...Danny's room."

"No, it's not...it's our new exercise room."

"But what about Danny? What if he comes home?"

Judith took hold of Penny's shoulders. "There is no Danny. Danny's gone. Do you understand?"

2025 City of Gold

Penny broke away from her mother's grasp. "I'll never go in that room. You have no right...it's Danny's." She ran blindly toward the stable. *What was wrong with Mom? How could she act like Danny was dead?* He wasn't dead. She didn't have a right to erase him.

Penny saddled Daniel's horse, Sandy. "It's okay, boy. Danny will be back someday." She let the horse break into a gallop, oblivious to the fact that she had no water or food with her. She headed north with only one thought in mind— to find Dad and the herd. Finally, she spotted the herd but her dad's truck was nowhere in sight. *Where are you, Dad?* She'd wait. Maybe he'd gone to get lunch or supplies. She panicked as she looked around, discovering no water for Sandy. She studied the area looking for signs of her dad's campsite but found no trace of a campfire. *That was weird.*

She tied her horse to a Palo Verde tree, sat down at its base, and bawled. Evil thoughts about her mother swirled through her mind. First, her mother didn't even listen to Grandpa and Grandma's warning. Then she sneaked off when everyone was worried about Grandma Jenny's stroke and got the "buy-sell number." Penny's thoughts raged. She'd even tried to spin the Ascension as historic and wonderful, and all it had done was kill Grandma and Grandpa.

What was wrong with her? Why did she think everything the government did was so cool? She was gaga over the president but treated Dad badly. Getting rid of Danny's room was the last straw.

Harry pulled off the road, heading for the herd. He'd finish their shots before he went back to the ranch. At least that part of his story would be true. He stopped the truck surprised to see Penny.

"Pen, what are you doing here?"

"Waiting for you, Dad. You'll never believe what Mom is doing."

Nothing Judith did surprised Harry anymore. He raised his eyebrows. "Go on."

"She's made an exercise room out of Danny's bedroom. Where is he s'posed to go when he comes back?" Tears flooded down Penny's cheeks.

Anger flared in Harry as he put his arm around his daughter. "I'm afraid he won't be back, Pen. He's considered a dissident. Do you know what that means?"

Penny shook her head.

"He didn't do what the government wanted. You might as well know. No one knows where Daniel is."

"Somebody knows."

"Somebody knows but doesn't want us to know. We received a letter telling us not to look for him."

"But you did, didn't you, Dad?"

"Yes, I did but I didn't find him. You can't get into the City of Gold."

"Do you think they put him in some dissident prison?"

"That's my thought, Penny."

"Thanks for being straight with me, Dad."

"You're welcome, kiddo. The exercise room is just your mother's way of handling her disappointment."

"How could she do it, Dad? It's like saying Danny's dead."

"He is to her. He's disappointed her. She feels he's made a huge mistake. She won't talk about Daniel and doesn't want me to either." He looked into Penny's distressed face. "You can always talk about Danny with me."

"Do you think he made a big mistake, Dad?"

"He followed his heart. It ruined his career with the government, but I think it was a true decision for Daniel. There's a lot you don't know, Penny, but Daniel is a very good person and I trust his judgment."

"Oh, Dad, I didn't bring any water for Sandy." Penny looked sheepish.

Harry took Sandy's lead and handed it to Penny. "There's a cave with a little pool of water over there where the mesquite are growing. We can set up camp there and give the horses a drink. I've got lots of food left from my trip. It's too late for you to ride home alone. Let's make a campfire and spend the night. In the morning you can help me give the herd the antibiotics and then we'll head home."

Penny gathered dead branches for their fire. Coyotes howled in the background.

"Scared?"

"Not with you here, Dad."

"Pen, there's something I need to talk to you about. Maybe this is a good time."

Penny gave him her full attention.

"Daniel told me that the government is offering scholarships to fifteen-year-old girls to spend a year away."

"I know about that program. One of my older friends is going on it. She gets to go to any Arizona university free."

"Do you know what happens on her year away?"

"No, no one talks about that. Peggy, our head cheer-leader, went this year but she doesn't want to cheer anymore. She cries in school and seems very sad."

"Danny's job was to escort girls from the Phoenix area to the year-away program."

"Danny?"

"Yes, he told me his doctor at the Center for New Age Medicine planted babies in the girls. Then Danny drove them to a health spa where they spent nine months while they were pregnant. Sometimes he drove the girls home."

"But they aren't married. Peggy didn't even have a boyfriend."

"They're using the president's sperm, Pen. He's the father of all the babies."

Penny grew quiet. "That doesn't seem right, does it, Dad? Shouldn't your first baby be with someone you love — your own husband?"

Harry smiled. At least Penny's head was thinking normally.

Penny frowned, "Will Mom want me to do the 'year away'?"

"Probably. She'll think a free university education is another wonderful gift from the president."

"Do I have to?"

"No, sweetheart, you don't. It's a year before the school will ask you."

"Does anyone ever say no?"

That question hadn't entered Harry's mind. He didn't know the answer. "I'll do my best to protect you, honey."

Penny looked up. "You may have to protect me from Mom."

Chapter Eighteen

J erry loaded the plane with the homeless, keeping one eye on Sebastian. Sebastian…a wonder Jerry got his name out of him since the guy hadn't spoken two sentences since Jerry picked him up. But…quiet was all right. The guy probably didn't want to draw attention since he was a dissident. Jerry signaled the Guardian to come aboard pointing to the co-pilot seat.

"Buckle up, kid, and we'll be off."

"Name's Rick Hathaway. Know your name is Jerry. Who's your helper?"

"Just a prisoner with muscles."

"What's your cargo scheduled for next week?" Rick asked as he buckled up.

"Nothing for you to worry about." The Guardian's know-it-all attitude irritated Jerry. Next week's cargo would be wooden caskets scheduled for Leavenworth but it was none of the kid's business. "You got new duty at Leavenworth?"

"Yeah, I'm looking forward to it. The closer I get to the City of Gold, the better I'll like it."

So this kid was a Guardian with a plan. "Next stop to be a Guardian at City of Gold, right?"

"That's my plan."

"It's no picnic, kid. Serious stuff going on at Leavenworth. You sure you're ready for the change? You look like someone who likes the good life."

Rick nodded. "I'm ready."

Jerry busied himself with takeoff, leaving Rick with his own thoughts. The Guardians puzzled Jerry. He'd witnessed MPs who used their military training to brutally deal with the dissidents. On the other hand, he remembered the poor kid he'd picked up at Fort Thompson. The reputation of the Guardians at Leavenworth was that they were a mean bunch. Jerry'd seen them push around a lot of people and even heard they'd shot a couple of homeless who got too close to the fence. He hoped Sebastian kept his head down. All he didn't need was this kid challenging him trying to score by bringing in another dissident.

Jerry began his descent, glad to end this flight. What was his life coming to carrying poor homeless people to Leavenworth? The plane landed and Rick started to herd the captured homeless off the plane.

"My cargo, kid. Just take care of your own business."

Rick stared at Sebastian. "Your helper was one of the guys I picked up the other night. I recognize him. He's a dissident, doesn't have the mark." Rick grabbed Sebastian pushing him off the plane. "No free ride for you, mister. I'm turning you in."

Jerry thought about fighting for the poor homeless man but decided to play dumb, opting not to get in trouble. He shook his head at Sebastian and saw his shoulders droop like a caged animal. "Sorry, man...I tried." Jerry stepped out of the way. "Don't have a way of checking their arm for the number. Thought he was just an ordinary homeless guy with a few muscles. Go ahead and take him. He's yours."

Rick prodded the homeless man, turning him over to the Guardian in charge.

"New MP? Second door to the left. Captain Giovanni will assign you to duty." Turning to Sebastian, he said, "Come with me."

Sebastian followed the Guardian to an office where he was cuffed and shoved into a chair. "Religious zealot?" The Guardian looked up.

"No. Just missed the time for getting the number."

"And how'd that happen? You had six months."

Sebastian had nothing to lose by answering the Guardian. "My wife had ovarian cancer; I was taking care of her. Lost track of everything. Lost my job, home, bank account…you got the picture?"

"What was your job?"

"Developing chips for Intel."

The Guardian took notes. The guy was interesting. Maybe the Prophet could use him. If so, he would certainly earn favor with the Prophet. Meantime he assigned Sebastian to a cell where he'd realize any offer from the Prophet beat the regular fate of the illegal dissident.

Obsessed with the fate of Lydia, Daniel kept running scenarios through the night, unable to sleep. He knew she must be terrified to be in a real prison. *Who were their fellow prisoners? Would he ever see her again? What would she be asked to do?* He felt heartsick.

At six a.m. the cell doors clanged open and a line formed. Used to the military, Daniel got in line behind a gray-haired man with stooped shoulders. The Guardian on duty led the line to a latrine. "Five minutes...clean up."

Daniel took the cheap toothbrush and soap, hurriedly washing up. *Would he see Lydia?*

The guard signaled the prisoners to follow him. In the prison cafeteria, Daniel received a bowl filled with a gray gruel and a cup of black coffee.

The prisoners in the cafeteria bore no resemblance to criminals. Daniel turned to ask the gray-haired man next to him about his life but the man lowered his head, refusing to communicate. A minute later, the guard on duty motioned Daniel to follow him.

"You're on latrine duty, kid. We got vermin in here. Scrub it clean." The soldier thrust bleach, noxious soap, and a brush into Daniel's hands and left, locking Daniel into the sewer of a bathroom. He sighed and started to work, the chlorine stinging his lungs and eating his hands. At least while he scrubbed, he didn't think.

Lydia awoke to find an older woman bending over her. "Don't be afraid of me, dear. My name's Elizabeth." She reached down and helped Lydia to her feet. Tears welled up in her eyes. "They really did a number on you, didn't they?"

Lydia felt violated. She searched the woman's eyes and saw a well of kindness. She nodded.

"They'll be marching us down to breakfast soon. I work the lunch shift. I'll try to get you on with me. It's the safest place to work. Would you like that?"

Lydia nodded again.

"I'm afraid this breakfast is only dreadful oatmeal with a few ants in it, but eat it. It'll keep your bones together. I won't ask you any questions now, but maybe later we can talk."

Lydia hated going to the bathroom in front of prisoners and guards. It seemed so primitive. She followed Elizabeth, repeating whatever the older woman did. Armed with a bowl of oatmeal, she sat down. "My name is Lydia." The old woman patted her hand. Elizabeth was the only light in this dirty, old prison.

Lydia wondered if she would ever see Daniel again. What a fool she'd been to think that the administration would send her and Daniel home. Following Daniel she'd entered a nightmare. *How could the president who'd created such a beautiful city allow them to be thrust into this dreadful prison? Who was he? Or rather who was the Prophet?*

Chapter Nineteen

Justin Prophet boarded the small military helicopter waiting to take him to Leavenworth. He'd done his homework finding an old federal prison—Leavenworth—a few miles from the City of Gold. The prison, originally an old fort, was a perfect place for the two thousand dissidents he'd already placed there. With the addition of the people who refused to accept the number, he was running out of room. His new organ donor initiative took care of two problems. It rid Omega I of unwanted guests who could not go back into society and provided the country with a supply of donor organs. The Prophet smiled; he didn't intend to keep people alive at the nation's expense. As the plane descended, the Prophet noticed the large cemetery bordering Leavenworth waiting for his new heroes and heroines. And…he did have Dr. Hart.

Greg Hart, coughed then spit the thick mucus that choked him. *Was it day or night? How long had he been in this moss-covered stone cell?* He ran his fingers across the damp wall reading the marks like he'd read Braille. Six rows and a mark for each day—forty-two. Six weeks? *Had he lived in this cell for six weeks?*

He'd prayed once and since that time he felt a Presence with him, not that it had gotten him out of the cold, dark prison, but the prayer gave him peace.

His mind jumped around refusing to let him think in a focused way. *Did his nurse make it to Rancho Christo? What happened to the Guardian who'd helped him take people there?* He lay back on the dirt floor.

What did he learn in the Army to keep his sanity in the hands of the enemy…a trip. He'd relive another trip. Where should he go today? Perhaps China. He remembered the trip he'd made for People to People, fifty doctors touring Beijing, Shanghai, and Suchow. The Great Wall fascinated him—wide enough to build a house on, it stretched as far as the eye could see.

Despite the industrialization of China and the strange appearance of automobile companies, McDonalds, and Starbucks, the guides made it a point to show them artifacts of their ancient culture. He saw jade rocks so huge you couldn't value them, the mummified corpse of Mao Tse-tung under glass, and the ancient art of silk making. The cities teemed with people who'd left the communes to make their fortune in the cities. Roads and high-rise buildings vied with remote corners of the city where the odor of fried fish and urine reminded you of the old China.

He tried to stand up...to stretch, his head hitting the ceiling. A trickle of blood oozed over his brow. *How long since he'd showered?* The foul smell stung his nose—his own body odor. *When would life in this hole end, when he was dead?*

The trapdoor on the cell rattled and someone pushed a putrid liquid through the slot. Perhaps he'd eat it...perhaps not. Maybe he'd go on a food strike. *What was he saving himself for?* He no longer had doubts about Alex Blackstone, his so-called college friend. The president was a demon disguised as a man. Suddenly, everything went black and when Greg awoke, he realized he'd spilled the soup.

"Mr. President."

"Yes." The president turned to face the Prophet.

"Your friend...Dr. Hart."

"Go on. You've got him on ice?"

"No, actually I've got him in solitary confinement...the hole, trying to make him more amenable to our ways. I think I've just the solution for the good doctor."

"And that would be?"

"A new initiative. I'm going to let the dissidents clear their name, if they wish. They can donate their organs and their slate will be wiped clean."

"How does the doctor fit in?"

"I need a surgeon."

Alex looked out over the City of Gold. He'd admired Greg Hart in college, so serious and dedicated. He'd hoped to include him in his plans. "What makes you think he'd consent to becoming our surgeon?"

"A choice...work for us or..." the Prophet made a slash across his throat.

"Where do you have him?"

"He's in Leavenworth with the dissidents. He's been in the hole for six weeks. I know he's still alive. How strong do you think his desire to live is?"

"I'm not sure. I've never understood the man. Very altruistic. Is there some way we could make him think he's helping mankind?"

The Prophet rolled his eyes. "Why don't I let you handle him."

"All right, I'll have a go at it. When will you be ready for him?"

"As soon as the surgery is built and the graves are dug. A few weeks at most."

"Shall I bring him in now?"

"Your call."

Unbelievably, the door to the hole was unlocked. Two huge hands picked Greg up and pulled him out the opening. The bright sunlight caused excruciating pain in his eyes. He closed them, blinded by the light. He needed darkness. "Where are you taking me?" he asked the guard.

"The president wants to see you."

"The president? Omega I?"

"Yes, Omega I." With that answer the guard handcuffed Dr. Hart and marched him onto a waiting helicopter.

Omega I looked up at the Phi Beta Kappa doctor before him, dirty, tattered, but still alive. "My friend, Dr. Hart, you honor me. Sit down." Omega I poured him a glass of red wine. The two sat staring at one another. "I take it you've not been comfortable. Would you like that to change?"

Greg didn't know what to say. He had so many questions.

Omega I handed him a clipping showing the headlines: *"Terrorists Kill Doctor in Car Bomb Accident."*

Greg read the headlines—so that was how they'd handled it.

"I have new work for you, a new initiative, so to speak."

Greg shuddered. *What kind of work could this demon have thought up for a dead doctor?* He waited.

"Since you were running your own little 'save the people' campaign, I thought you might like a more altruistic job. We have a new initiative and we need a surgeon—a good surgeon. The dissidents condemned to die are being held in Leavenworth—your former home. To clear their names, they may volunteer for a program to donate their organs for transplants—their choice, of course." Omega I waited.

"But they are alive."

"That's where you come in, Doctor. You put them to sleep, remove their organs, and make heroes out of them."

And what if I won't do this?"

"I don't know if an already dead doctor's organs can be used, but perhaps you would like to find out."

As Greg digested the offer, he saw total evil in the president's eyes.

"You can sleep on it. You'll be given a good meal, a suite for the night, fresh clothes, and a shower. Feel free to walk around. You are in the City of Gold—a highly secure creation. See if you'd like to change your mind, doctor. The choice as always is yours. Here is a dining pass. The octagon building with the rotating tower holds the restaurant. After you clean up, please be our guest. You are dismissed."

Greg needed no time to decide. From the moment Alex proposed the opportunity, he knew what his answer would be. But at least he'd clean up, have a meal on the house, and get a good night's sleep. He showered and trimmed his beard, putting on a clean, odorless shirt and pair of slacks. The pain of going from dark to light still stunned him. He sauntered around the City of Gold, amazed at its beauty.

The golden statue of Omega I addressed him. "Dr. Hart, isn't it? Surgeon to Omega I?"

Greg ignored the statue, stunned at its powers of discernment. The streets intrigued him with the blue waters babbling and flowing under the crystal streets. He was also surprised to find young people in the city. He chose the escalating stairs to the top of the octagonal building, showed his

2025 City of Gold

guest pass, and was escorted to a solitary dining table overlooking the city.

Tomorrow...tomorrow...but tonight he'd eat like a king. Oddly, he wasn't afraid. *Was he eating his last meal?* His attention turned to the media broadcast shown on monitors throughout the dining room. The world grew darker and darker. He watched news of beheadings in the Arab countries for dissidents who didn't accept the new world religion, earthquakes, fires, and floods. A 9.5 earthquake in Mexico showed thousands of people buried under buildings and there he sat—Dr. Greg Hart eating a lobster while imprisoned in the City of Gold.

Omega I awaited Dr. Hart's entrance. What fate would the good doctor choose? To cooperate or, like the other dissident fools, would he choose extinction? The Prophet informed him that another surgeon from Boston was honored to head the new initiative. Hart's response didn't matter. The Prophet referred to the new surgeon as the "Boston butcher." Alex leaned back in his chair, appreciative of the fact that the Prophet handled all details of the dissidents. What would he do without the Prophet's brilliant schemes to eliminate troublemakers?

Dr. Hart awoke with a deep peace. His answer would be "no." It would give him pleasure to register that decision to Alex, personally. He dressed and followed the guards to the president's office where Alex and the Prophet waited for him.

"Well," challenged the Prophet.

Greg turned to Alex. "My old friend, I'm sorry to disappoint you, but..."

The president turned away. Two Guardians removed Greg. Dr. Hart was about to die for the second time.

Chapter Twenty

J erry landed the helicopter on the dirt road next to the shack where the carpenter lived who worked for the government, building cheap wooden caskets. Hearing an electric saw, Jerry walked out to the barn. His assignments grew weirder and weirder. This guy made cheap coffins which Jerry flew to Leavenworth at least twice a week. By now, he'd flown over a hundred coffins and something told him there'd be more.

"Hey, Mac, you want to help me load these works of art on Old Glory?"

"Let me finish this one, Jerry. What are they planning to do with all these coffins?"

"Beats me. I drop them off near the cemetery at Leavenworth. No one seems to know what or who they're for. Something's going down soon though. I can feel it in my bones. Say, could I borrow your old truck to make a run in to see my mom?"

"Help yourself. The old truck's got gas but she's not too dependable."

Jerry thanked Mac, took the truck keys, and started the motor, his spirits lifting at the thought of having a nice supper with his mom and spending the night. He rolled up to the curb of the small, ancient Sun City dwelling, happy to see his mom watering her flowers.

"Hey, Mom, got some supper for me?" Jerry lifted her off her feet with a big bear hug.

"Always, Jerry. I'm surprised to see you."

Jerry explained he had a run nearby and wanted to see how she was doing. She smiled and waved him inside. "Same as usual, Jerry. I made some chicken enchiladas yesterday and put a couple in the freezer. Does that sound all right?"

"You know I love your enchiladas, Ma. Bring 'em on."

The two sat down, enjoying just being together. "What did you really come for, son?"

Jerry's mom always amazed him at how she could read him. "I need your advice, Mom."

Jerry told her about the runs he'd been making and the coffins. Then he asked her if she had a picture or could describe the doc at the Center for New Age Medicine who'd helped her.

She opened a drawer in her lamp stand and pulled out a faded newspaper picture of Dr. Hart that had appeared in the paper when his car was bombed.

Jerry was dumbfounded. The picture was of the guy he'd just delivered to the City of Gold and was told to pick up tomorrow on his way back to Leavenworth. Even as dirty and beat up as he'd been when Jerry delivered him, he still resembled the faded picture.

"Mom, you know I have a deal with the government to make runs for them and they'll keep you out of the Ascension. I've never kept that from you."

"No, you haven't. You hate these runs though; I've known it for a long time."

"There's some real dark stuff going on, Mom. They're filling up that old federal prison with dissidents. Now they're having me bring coffins by the hundreds. Taking planeloads of plants to the City of Gold is one thing but...I don't know how long I can keep working for them."

"Jerry, you don't have to work for the president if it steals your life. I'm old now and the thought of dying doesn't scare me. We're born to die. What are you thinking?"

"I think I have to pick up the doc when I leave here. They must have killed off a homeless man with the car bomb. I'd like to help him get away from them but it would be dangerous. I'm fed up. They'd kill me for doin' it so I might not make it back here. I don't want to put you in danger." Jerry thought out loud. "Unless, somehow I could pick you up and get you out of Sun City where you'd be safe."

"Help the doc, Jerry. He helped a lot of us. He's a good man."

"If you promise to leave your house and go stay with a friend. I can't let you be in danger, Ma. Will you do that for me?"

"What if I just tell them I haven't seen you and have no idea where you are?"

Jerry shook his head. "I think they'd hold you hostage."

Jerry left, undecided as to whether he'd have the courage to cross the Prophet.

Chapter Twenty-one

T hanks to Elizabeth, Lydia was assigned to work in the kitchen. Every day she watched for Daniel to come through her line. Then one morning he did. Their eyes met and tears flowed down both their cheeks. They'd shaved Daniel's head and he'd grown a beard of sorts. His shocked eyes told her what he thought of her appearance. She tried to smile, to hide her heartbreak.

"Lydia...I'm so sorry."

"I know, Daniel."

She'd watched for Daniel each day, longing for just a few minutes, a few kind words but when they switched Lydia to work lunches, she never saw him.

"Elizabeth, do we ever get to be with the men?"

"In the exercise area, but if your friend is assigned to a labor crew he'll be working through lunch. And he won't show up in the exercise area. They tell me some of the strong men are assigned to work crews."

Finished with serving lunch, Lydia and Elizabeth followed the prisoners to the area designated for exercise. "Don't look at the guards, dear. Keep your eyes down."

Lydia slipped her arm inside Elizabeth's to support her as they walked. "How did you end up in prison, Elizabeth?"

"I couldn't take the number to buy and sell. I lived alone and my landlord reported me before I could find a place to go. I follow the old ways," sighed the woman.

"What are the old ways? What do you mean?" asked Lydia.

"I live my life by the Bible. The Bible warns that at some time in the world, we will be asked to take a number to buy and sell. Christians cannot take this number. It is the number of the lawless one—the Antichrist."

Lydia thought about Elizabeth's words. "What do you know about the lawless one?"

"He is a man who gains power and makes his own laws and rules, thinking he is a god. Doesn't that sound a little like our president? He has no use for our Constitution or the ten commandments that our country was founded on. He makes up laws as he goes."

"I didn't grow up with religion," Lydia said. "My family is Jewish. My great grandparents were gassed in the holocaust. My parents are good people but not religious. Tell me why so many people today risk their lives to follow the teachings in the Bible?"

Elizabeth looked at Lydia. "Because Jesus will be coming back soon. Of course, you know Jesus was a Jew and so were many of his first disciples. He is God's son and God sent Him into the world to pay the price for our wrongs."

"Did the people of His times think he was the Messiah?" Lydia asked. "I think the Jews today are still waiting for the Messiah—a savior."

"The religious people of His day and the Romans killed Jesus. Three days after His death, He arose from the dead. If we believe in Jesus and follow His ways, we will go to heaven. If we take the number, we become the enemy of God."

"Tell me about Jesus."

"He healed the deaf, the blind, lepers, paralyzed people, and even raised three people that we know of from the dead."

Lydia's eyes glistened. "Like the Prophet?"

"No dear, not like the Prophet. The Prophet only raised one man, the president. Evil can work miracles sometimes too. I believe both he and the Prophet are evil. Look around you. These people aren't criminals. They are good people, many who wouldn't take the number and wanted to worship God like me. We are here in prison because of the Prophet and the president."

Chapter Twenty-two

Daniel Jordan's disappearance changed Rick Hathaway's future forever. He hated every minute he worked for the Center for New Age Medicine but when Dr. Hart transferred him to the Guardian Military Police, he felt free, let out of prison. Rick wondered why the good doctor had been eliminated by a car bomb—a familiar means of getting rid of your enemies in New Jersey where he was from. Had the doctor crossed Omega I?

One thing Rick understood, no one got away with crossing either the president or the Prophet. Those who opposed the new world they were designing ended up in prison or worse.

So far Rick's duty at Leavenworth was routine: placing new prisoners into cells, guarding the exercise area, and waiting on the Prophet when he visited. The Prophet even knew his name. The way Rick figured it, the Prophet controlled the destiny of the dissidents, an area his MP skills excelled in. Someday he planned to be part of the Prophet's inner circle. Rick thought the dissidents must be brainless to refuse the new system. Rumor circulated among the guards that soon the dissidents would be executed. To Rick, the dissidents weren't people—they were the enemy. As the enemy, he no longer had to handle them with kid gloves. Determined to earn a position in the City of Gold, Rick was ruthless with prisoners, getting himself named "The Nazi" by the prisoners, now afraid of him.

Rick reminded himself to be patient. He missed the night life of Phoenix. He'd traded a winter of 50 to 70 degrees for a bleak, gray world with temperatures below zero. The only entertainment—an occasional game of poker with the other guards.

From the Guardian lookout tower, Rick scanned the grassless enclosure where the inmates walked. No one tried to escape, afraid they would be shot. He glimpsed an old white-haired woman walking with what appeared to be a young boy. On second glance, Rick realized the old woman walked with a girl. Her hair was chopped off in the style of new arrivals but her body was good. He studied her face with binoculars, surprised to find pretty features. A few pounds, a better haircut, and some makeup, and she'd be all right.

Rick knew he was handsome. Perhaps the girl would be grateful for better food and a few hours out of her cell. He had needs. He was young and virile. Excited, Rick formed a plan. First, he'd find out the girl's cell number. Then he'd offer her chocolate, fresh fruit, and his company at night. He'd wine and dine her and return her to her cell before roll call. They would both benefit.

Elizabeth looked up catching sight of a guard looking at Lydia with binoculars. That meant only one thing—trouble.

A key rattled in the cell door catching Lydia and Elizabeth off guard. A Guardian entered the cell, taking Lydia by her hand and leading her out the door. *Had she done something wrong?* She studied the guard. He smiled at her, leading her down the hallway and finally stopping at a room. He opened the door and led her into what appeared to be his room. On a small table, she saw fresh fruit and chocolate. A TV showed a movie she'd seen once in a theater in San Diego. *Why was she here?*

Rick sat down on his bed, patting the mattress beside him but Lydia didn't move.

"You don't have to be afraid. I'm a friend. Would you like some chocolate or fruit?"

Lydia still did not move, fear running through her veins. *What did he really want?* "What do you want, sir? Have I done something wrong?"

Rick laughed heartily. "No, no. You've done nothing wrong. I just want to be your friend. I hope we can help one another. I have needs. You have needs. Right? We can help each other."

Lydia backed up. "No, I can't help you."

"Listen, Lydia, I don't want to hurt you. You are sentenced for life in prison. Wouldn't a few nights out of your cell, some real food, and entertainment make your life more tolerable?"

What did he mean she was in prison for life?

Lydia remained silent, aware the Guardian could overpower her easily. She looked into Rick's eyes and saw that he wanted affection. She was afraid. "I don't know you. I'm not like that. Please take me back to my cell."

Rick hesitated, not wanting to scare the girl. Perhaps if he developed a friendship with her, she'd see that he could help her have a better life in prison. He opened his door and led her back to her cell. "Let's start over. My name is Rick. I'll be back tomorrow night. We'll have dinner, a drink, and talk."

Lydia entered her cell. Rick left. Elizabeth got up off her knees. "I was praying for you Lydia. Are you all right?"

"The Guardian wants to give me extra food and entertainment for favors." Lydia looked down. "He said I was in prison for life and he wanted to make my life a little better." Lydia threw herself on her bed sobbing. "What should I do, Elizabeth? He's coming back tomorrow. If only I could get a message to Daniel. I don't know what to do."

Chapter Twenty-three

Transferred to a building crew, Daniel worked dawn to dusk on a small building located in the woods on the prison property. The building contained three rooms, two with operating tables and one with five or six refrigerated units. The building appeared to be a modern clinic for surgery. If so, where were the hospital beds and why wasn't there a recovery room? Did they expect to send a new surgery back into the cold, damp, moldy cells? It didn't make sense.

When he arrived back at his cell, he found he'd gained a cellmate. The man appeared to be in his forties with salt-and-pepper hair. The prison held powerful people—constitutional lawyers, outspoken media critics, Christian broadcasters and ministers, as well as people who wouldn't take the number to buy and sell. The man looked at him with deep, sad eyes and Daniel wondered what his story was.

"Welcome to Leavenworth, the name's Daniel."

"Sebastian Cramer."

Daniel sank down on his cot, exhausted from twelve hours of lifting heavy lumber and installing the lab equipment. "Is this your first day?"

"Yeah." Neither wanted to break the ice with a long discourse. Sebastian eyed the young man, judging him to be around twenty. "What did you do, kid, to get in here?"

"Long story. How 'bout you?"

Sebastian wrestled with whether to confide in the kid or just stay to himself. Finally, when Daniel had given up on an answer, Sebastian surprised him by talking. "My wife Callie got uterine cancer; she was the best thing in my life. I quit my job at Intel so I could take care of her. I guess I shut the world out. I just wanted to have every minute with Callie. The day she died, I was holding her hand. She reached up and touched my face. Her last words were, 'Don't stop living, Sebastian, because of me.'"

"But why are you here?" Daniel asked.

"No number. I didn't get the number."

"How did you live?"

Sebastian looked at Daniel. "I'm not really living, kid. No job, no house, no access to my financial accounts. Homeless. Then I got lucky and was picked up by some Guardians who saw I didn't have the number to buy and sell. And here I am. What do I have to look forward to?"

"Not much. Enough food to barely keep you alive, my company at night, and a dismal cell."

"Do we work?"

"We do. I'm on a work crew building a small medical clinic. You look healthy so I'm sure they'll put you on some kind of labor. Tomorrow I'm assigned to dig graves."

Sebastian looked up, many questions in his eyes. "Digging graves? For whom?"

"Probably for some of us."

"So how does a young person end up in a dissident prison?"

Daniel lay down and closed his eyes. "I was a Guardian; got sent to be a Youth Council member to the City of Gold."

"The new capital?"

"Yes. At first it was a magical place. The Youth Council was assigned to propose initiatives to change the educational system but really, they brainwashed us, giving us the good life, preparing us to return as ambassadors to our home states to rave about the new system."

"What happened?"

"I guess you had to be there. There's this golden statue of the president which is probably programmed with everyone in the city's history—a computerized robot that somehow thinks on its own. On the day the new capital was shown to the public via satellite, the Youth Council was asked to bow before this mechanical wonder and pledge our lives in allegiance—a test of obedience."

"That was a problem?"

"It was. I couldn't do it. I wasn't going to bow and pledge my life to a golden statue. It was a loyalty test. I failed and my friend Lydia stayed with me. That's the hard part for me. I never see her and the only chance I get is when she works the kitchen. If they give me time off, the men and women do get to be in the exercise area together. So far that hasn't happened."

"What's her name?"

"Lydia...Lydia Cohen."

Suddenly the most beautiful soft singing interrupted their conversation, weaving from cell to cell filling the halls and echoing off the walls.

"It sounds like music sung by monks." Sebastian lay back on his bunk and closed his eyes. "Who would be singing in this cold, hopeless prison?"

Daniel listened. "The Christians…they sing hymns every night for about a half hour."

The following night Daniel returned soaked to the skin, caked with mud and shaking.

"Hey, buddy, what happened to you?" Sebastian asked.

"We're digging graves and it rained all day." Daniel sank down on his cot so weary and aching he didn't even want to try to lie down."

"Daniel, what does your friend Lydia look like?"

"She has dark hair, gray-blue eyes. She's beautiful but they chopped her hair off. Why?"

"I think she was working lunch. Then we went outdoors to the exercise area. She walked around with a white-haired older woman. Would that be her?"

"Yes."

"I was afraid of that. One of the guards had his binoculars trained on her the whole time we were in there. I didn't want to scare her but I think the guard looking at her like that means trouble."

Distressed, Daniel jumped to his feet. "What can I do?"

Sebastian was quiet. "I'll take your duty digging graves tomorrow. I doubt they'll care. You go into the exercise area. See if I'm right."

Daniel had nothing to lose. Sebastian's offer to dig graves overwhelmed him. The guy would do that for him?

The next morning when the guard came for Daniel, Sebastian stepped up to take his place. The guard ignored the switch. Daniel waited and left the cell with the other prisoners heading for breakfast and the exercise area. Lydia and the white-haired woman were walking slowly. Daniel fell in step behind them.

"Lydia, it's Daniel."

Shocked Lydia turned around. "Daniel, I haven't seen you since the first day."

"I know." Daniel put his arm around her shoulder. "Are you all right?"

"No—" Just then they were interrupted by a Guardian pulling Lydia away from Daniel.

Without thinking, on reflex Daniel shoved the Guardian. A sharp crack from above knocked him off his feet. He grabbed his leg and stood up. Weak from lack of food and digging graves, he still remembered some of the deadly Shotokan moves. If he was going to die, he'd die protecting Lydia. "Leave her alone."

The voice caught Rick off guard. *Who did this guy think he was?* The voice sounded familiar. *Was the man married to this girl?*

The last thing Rick wanted was trouble or attention on what he was doing. He signaled the guard that he was okay and in charge. He wouldn't risk his position for this pathetic girl. "I have no interest in her. Get back," he ordered.

Then in one lightning moment, Daniel recognized Rick and Rick recognized Daniel. Immediately Daniel understood why Rick was interested in Lydia. While on duty, Rick spotted Lydia and, of course, his animal instincts kicked in.

Not wanting Daniel to recognize him, Rick turned away. He did not acknowledge Daniel—Daniel was the enemy. The enemy had no names. Further, in Daniel's rundown condition, he was no match for Rick. "Better have that ankle checked out," Rick said.

"Oh, Daniel, you're bleeding."

Rick returned to his quarters. *Well, that solves the mystery of Daniel Jordan,* he thought. And suddenly, Rick felt powerful and important. In the end, he'd beaten Daniel. It felt good, really good, even better than taking the girl. He wouldn't bother her again—it would be his only recognition of his old partner. And...his debt to Daniel would be paid in full.

Chapter Twenty-four

J erry's mother did not understand the danger she'd be in without Jerry's protection. Unable to leave her in Sun City, he made another attempt to convince her to come with him.

"Mom, let's have this conversation again. You can't stay in Sun City. You need to come with me. We'll start over in Canada and I'll take care of you. How soon can you pack and be ready?"

"But Jerry—"

"No 'but Jerry.' It's too dangerous for you to remain in Sun City if I quit my job. I think I can work for the forestry department in Canada. We'll get a little cabin up north. What do you say, Mom?"

Jerry waited while his mother thought it over. "All right, Jerry. I'll miss my friends and my flowers but I know this means a lot to you. I'll just put a few clothes together."

Jerry waited as his mother threw some clothes in a bag and closed up her house. He helped her up into the old truck and they headed back to pick up the coffins, his final delivery. He'd already received a text message from the Prophet notifying him that a prisoner needed to be returned to Leavenworth. It had to be Dr. Hart.

He hated to leave his mother with the carpenter but, after thinking it over, that seemed the safest plan. He'd deliver the coffins, return to the City of Gold and collect the doctor, and then pick up his mother. He knew Mac, the carpenter, would take good care of her and probably experience some good home cooking while Jerry was gone.

Jerry set the helicopter down next to the cemetery, amazed that over one hundred graves waited to be filled. *What was going down? Why the caskets and the graves? Was the Prophet going to have the dissidents killed?* The Guardians herded a few prisoners over to unload the helicopter. "Hey guys," Jerry yelled at the Guardians. "What goes with all the graves?"

"Making room for more dissidents, I guess. Prophet's got a new initiative," said one of the Guardians. "He's cleaning house."

Two Guardians pushed Dr. Hart roughly into the waiting helicopter. Jerry held his breath, hoping the doctor was his only passenger.

"Sit up here, doc," said Jerry, pointing to the empty co-pilot seat.

The doctor took his seat, buckling himself in. He judged the pilot to be mid-sixties, bearded, his faded Hawaiian shirt barely covering a pronounced beer belly. The helicopter was ancient, but functioning. "You know who I am?"

"Yeah, doc, I do. You're the dead doc who got blown up in a car bomb accident by our very own terrorists...the Prophet and company. Am I right?"

"Right on. And now I'm to be the first dead doc to die again, giving his organs to someone in Phoenix."

"Afraid not. Change of plans. You're the dead doc who's about to resurrect from the dead and join me and my mom in Canada. Sound all right to you?"

Dr. Hart was speechless. "You prepared to be enemy Number 1?"

"I am. Figure I'll take my only living relative, my mom, with us and I'll hope for a job in the forestry department in Canada. We helicopter pilots with our own plane are kinda scarce these days. Maybe they can use me to put out fires or something."

Dr. Hart leaned back, closing his eyes totally unprepared for this change of events but thankful just the same. He wished the pilot could take him to Rancho Christo. Should he ask? After thinking about it, Dr. Hart decided staying in the country put Jerry in too much danger. He relaxed and asked him if he knew safe houses for dissidents existed all over the country and probably even in Canada?"

"No, doc, I didn't but we're two valuable people you and I. Someone can use our skills, right?"

"All prisoners report to the indoor exercise area. I repeat...all prisoners." The electronic cell doors clanged open and men and women filed out, ushered to the indoor area. A large screen hung from wires surrounded by rusted metal chairs. Armed Guardians surrounded the room.

"Are we having a movie?" whispered Lydia to Elizabeth.

"No talking," a voice ordered.

The lights dimmed and the familiar face of Omega I filled the screen. "If you are watching this film, you are in prison condemned to die or sentenced to life imprisonment. Your presence here brings shame on your families. Today, I come to offer you a chance to redeem yourselves and help your country.

"The shortage for organ donors in the world has reached epidemic proportions. Many people need transplants— hearts, kidneys, lungs, and tissues. Now you have the opportunity to be a hero or a heroine.

"As condemned prisoners, you have no future. Your life will continue as it is until you are executed. This is the opportunity I am offering. If you volunteer as an organ donor, you will be put to sleep and your organs harvested. Your family's name will be restored. You will be buried with honor in a special cemetery for heroes. Your families will be awarded the presidential Medal of Valor awarded to civilians who risk their lives to save the lives of others and a special Flag of Valor. The choice is yours. Remember, there is no greater love than that one should give his life for another.

"A new surgical unit is completed here at Leavenworth. You will feel no pain. Your organs will be flown immediately to your home state. Think seriously about this offer. Would it not be better to die as a hero than as a criminal?"

Elizabeth noticed tears rolling down Lydia's cheeks. *What was she thinking?*

"Lydia? Are you all right?"

"I'm only twenty years old. I didn't realize we'd been sentenced to die. I didn't even realize we could be in prison for life. What did we do to deserve this?" Tears flooded her cheeks.

A few days later, Daniel soaked and covered with mud, rushed to the exercise area hoping to see Lydia. Rain had turned the grave digging into mud, making it impossible to work.

"Danny, where have you been?"

Daniel said nothing. He didn't want to tell Lydia he'd dug three graves in the rain and watched twenty people get buried today. He didn't want to tell her that he'd even resisted the idea of them being buried in the graves.

"I can't do this anymore," sobbed Lydia. "I told Elizabeth how frightened I am. She's been telling me about Jesus. Do you know about Jesus, Daniel?"

"Yes, my grandparents followed the old ways. Grandpa left me his Bible and I read about Jesus."

"Do you know He's coming soon?"

Daniel nodded. *Where was Lydia going with this?* "He died and went to heaven."

"But do you know He's coming to the world again soon?"

"Why are you telling me this, Lydia?"

"Elizabeth says that we can ask Jesus into our hearts. He'll live in us and give us strength for whatever comes. I want to be a follower of Jesus, Danny. Do you know He was Jewish, too? I think He is the Messiah that the Jewish people have been waiting for."

"Lydia, do you understand what's happening here? They buried twenty people in the graves I've been digging today. We're in terrible trouble. We don't have time for mystical beliefs. They take people every day from the cells and they don't come back."

Lydia looked deeply into Daniel's eyes. "That's exactly why I need Him. I need His strength. I can't make it by myself."

Daniel's heart was torn but the idea of a mystical Jesus living in their heart...? He wanted to put his arms around Lydia but his dirty clothes prevented him. "I know you're upset, honey. I can't blame you, but I can't follow Jesus. I've given my heart to my grandfather's God, the God of creation. When I was at Fort Thompson I asked Grandpa's God for help and He's my God. He saved my life."

"Daniel, they are one."

"I don't understand."

"Neither do I, Danny, but Elizabeth says they are one. She says that the God who created the world—she calls Him the Father—sent His only Son Jesus into the world to die for us...for our sins. The Father was in Jesus, and Jesus can live in our hearts through His Spirit, if we just ask."

"I know Jesus was a good and holy man but I didn't know that the Creator was his Father."

"Elizabeth says when we ask Jesus into our heart, his Holy Spirit comes like a seed of God to make us one with God."

"Do you believe this, Lydia?"

"Yes, I'm going to ask Him. What do we have to lose, Danny? If it isn't real, nothing will happen. But if she's right..."

Chapter Twenty-five

Daniel returned to his cell to find Sebastian sitting on the edge of his bed.

"Another day digging graves?" Sebastian asked without looking up.

"Yeah, I saw Lydia in the exercise area. She's losing hope. I don't know what to do. She's going to become a Christian."

"The little old lady is influencing her?"

"I guess. She's convinced Lydia if she asks Jesus into her heart, He'll come to live inside her. Have you ever heard of that?"

Sebastian lay back on his cot. "It's called being born again."

Daniel stood over Sebastian. "Then she's not hallucinating?"

"No, I was a born-again Christian until my wife died. Then I lost my faith. I couldn't understand why a good God would let my wife die. She was so young. When she died, so did my faith. But now...I don't know. There's evil in the world...disease ...earthquakes...maybe it makes God sad, too. That's what I'm beginning to think."

Daniel tried to digest what Sebastian said. "She said the God who created the world..."

"The Father. His Son is Jesus who is the image of His Father."

"But how can He—They—live in your heart?"

"It's a miracle. I'm a scientist but as a scientist I'm taught to experiment. So...I asked Jesus into my heart. If there was a God who created the world, who created us with all the systems working together inside us, why would I want to be without Him in my life?"

As Sebastian talked, his face lit up and hope and energy radiated from him. "We do need Him, Danny. Would you like to ask Him into whatever life you have left? I think I would like to talk to Him again. He used to put thoughts in my mind. And His big number is forgiveness."

A silence filled the cell as the two men quietly asked Jesus into their hearts...one for the first time. And one returning from a long, lonely trip.

Chapter Twenty-six

The dissident prison was highly guarded; there was no way out. Daniel ached for Lydia. She'd followed Daniel, worried when she saw the guards attack him. He wanted to pray but he didn't know how. How do you talk to God?

Talk to me, Daniel, I'm listening.

Is that what Sebastian meant when he said God put thoughts in your mind? *Father, can you help us? Is there any way to get out? Please, Lord, I know you protected my mind in Fort Thompson. Are you great enough to get us out of this fortress? Show us the way. We are going to die here. You are our only hope.*

The next day a guard came for Sebastian who followed him to a small office in the prison. There he was told to put on a clean pair of slacks, shirt, and shoes. *Where did they plan to take him?* After dressing, a Guardian shoved him onto a helicopter. Twenty minutes later, the helicopter landed through the glass dome of what Sebastian supposed was the City of Gold he'd heard so much about. The Guardian ushered him into the office of the Prophet.

"You are Sebastian Cramer? An ex-employee of Intel? Sit down, Mr. Cramer."

The stories Daniel told Sebastian about the Prophet didn't prepare him for the enormous cloud of evil that radiated from the man. "Yes, sir."

"Did your duty at Intel involve working with computer chips?'

"It did."

"I have a small problem with the president's golden statue. I think its hard drive is defective or something is wrong with the chip. You will help me with my problem and in return you will get a few days in the City of Gold. I will appoint a Guardian escort for you. While you are here, you may enjoy access to food, entertainment, and recreation.

Your focus will be to restore the virility of the golden statue. Is that understood?"

Sebastian nodded his head in acknowledgment. He followed the Guardian to a suite assigned to him. The Guardian left him with instructions to shower and said he'd return at seven p.m. to take him to dinner.

Sebastian turned on the media center. Global News Network was showing pictures of the old capital. He listened. "Worse than the 9/11 debacle—Washington, D.C. lies in ruins. The Pentagon blasted into a million pieces."

The satellite photography showed Arlington Cemetery where thousands of soldiers' gravestones lay uprooted—the cemetery desecrated. Nothing in the city remained, not even the White House. The narrator continued, "Terrorists have dealt the United States a death blow."

Sebastian walked into the shower. As the water washed over him, he remembered his habit of years past and prayed, *"Lord, wash away my doubts and fears. Forgive the months of unbelief. I need you now, Lord, in this dangerous place. Watch over me."*

For the first time in months, Sebastian felt free, totally unafraid of death. Death meant only one thing: Callie would be in his life again.

Hundreds of graves waited for the bodies of those who planned to donate their organs and clear their names. Daniel continued to dig. On bad weather days, he followed his fellow prisoners, able to spend a little time each day with Lydia. He explained what Sebastian told him about being "born again."

"Daniel, does that mean you asked Jesus into your heart?" asked Lydia.

Daniel smiled. "It does."

"I wish I knew more about Him."

"I'm sure Elizabeth knows lots of stories about Jesus. Ask her to fill you in."

"She wants to donate her organs, Danny. She says she's old and the thought of living in Leavenworth...she's fragile...it's too cold for her; this life is too hard." Lydia looked deeply into Daniel's eyes. "I understand what she's saying. I feel the same way. At least our family name would be restored."

A cold chill surrounded Daniel's heart. "Lydia, we're only twenty years old."

"But we have no life to look forward to, Danny. There is no way out of Leavenworth. At least we'd be together in heaven."

"He won't win, Lydia. In the last book in the Bible—the Revelation—it speaks of a lawless man who changes everything...is powerful...thinks he's a god. He doesn't win."

Lydia stopped. "Daniel, is that why you couldn't bow before the statue? You think Omega I is the lawless man?"

Chapter Twenty-seven

"Turn the sound up," said Harry, sitting on the edge of the couch. Pictures of a nuclear holocaust caught the family's attention. Smoke and debris littered the streets of D.C. A ticker-tape flashed across the bottom of the screen: "Washington, D.C. Attacked by a Nuclear Bomb."

The announcer's voice followed: "The Washington Monument, Jefferson's Memorial, the White House, Supreme Court, and the Pentagon wiped from the face of the earth." As the satellite picture grew closer, they saw pictures of tombstones upturned in Arlington Cemetery.

"Even the dead were not spared. The nuclear fallout in the old capital will kill anyone still living in the city."

"Radiation will prevent anyone from checking for survivors," said another announcer.

The Jordan family sat glued to the pictures crossing the TV before them.

"It's a good thing the new capital is bombproof and all our legislators are safe," said Judith.

Harry thought about that. Now all remnants of the America he knew and loved were gone. He listened as the announcers continued.

"Iran claims credit for the nuclear blast. We are waiting to hear from our president."

The cameras switched to the City of Gold where President Blackstone and Vice President Justin Prophet waited to make a statement.

"Fellow citizens, it is a sad day in our country. Our beloved capital and all its historical memorials are gone. Thousands of innocent people died in the nuclear explosion. Built to protect against just such nuclear attacks, I can only be thankful that our beautiful new capital keeps our government and legislators safe. Perhaps it is a time for America to really enter a new era. We must honor our dead but keep our focus on the future."

Off camera the Prophet spoke. "Terrorists were a bigger threat than we thought," he said.

Omega I turned to face him. "Amazing what a well-placed nuke can do to a city."

The Prophet frowned. "A well-placed nuke?"

Omega I sighed. "Just a little side deal with Iran. They get notoriety, we get oil."

The Prophet had underestimated the president. "You are saying *we* are responsible for the nuke hitting DC?"

"Makes the City of Gold even more precious, doesn't it? Now any fears of the Supreme Court coming to life, or the military rising up are put to rest. The American people will beg for protection and world peace."

Amazed that President Blackstone orchestrated the destruction of the old capital without consulting him, Justin Prophet had a new respect for his leader.

Chapter Twenty-eight

D aniel didn't like the fact that Elizabeth was influencing Lydia to think about donating her organs. But how could he discourage her from being friends with Elizabeth when Elizabeth had been almost a mother to her? Nevertheless, he didn't want her to follow Elizabeth if she decided to donate her organs. He hurried to meet Lydia in the exercise area.

"Danny," Lydia interrupted his thoughts. "The administration set the age at 65 for donating organs. Elizabeth is so disappointed. I'm afraid her health is failing, her cough is terrible and she may have pneumonia. I feel so sad for her."

Daniel didn't know how to comfort Lydia. "She's been a good friend."

"She's protected me." Lydia began to cry. "I still think we should donate our organs. At least we'd be together."

Startled, Daniel stopped walking and put his arm around Lydia. "Lydia, what are you saying? Maybe it's enough for me just being with you...even here. I can't do it, Lydia. Try to understand." Daniel watched as the light drained from her eyes.

Daniel surveyed the field where they were digging graves. The fog hadn't lifted but he could still see ten new graves with white markers and row after row of holes waiting for organ donors.

He shoveled dirt, feverishly angry with himself, Omega I...the Prophet...the Guardians...his mother...and the world in general. The rain pounded him, making it difficult to dig. He prayed that he and Lydia would not end their lives in one of these holes.

Later that night, Daniel lay shivering, exhausted, wet to the bone. He missed Sebastian. Gone for two nights, Daniel feared Sebastian might be in terrible trouble. What could the administration want with him?

Sebastian strolled around the City of Gold, awed by the engineering and design. Exotic plants followed the twisting waterway that wound its path throughout the city. When he arrived at the amphitheater with the revolving restaurant, the Guardian assigned to him was waiting for him and steered him to the luxurious buffet. They chose their food in silence, the Guardian watching Sebastian carefully.

"You don't look like the normal tourist, Sebastian. I'm curious; what did the Prophet bring you to the City of Gold to do?"

Sebastian hesitated, sensing the Guardian just tried to make conversation." I'm a chip expert. Hear there's trouble with the golden statue but haven't examined it yet. As you probably know, I'm a prisoner at Leavenworth. Long story. My understanding is that when I've finished my job here, I'll return to Leavenworth. Forgive me if I enjoy real food. And you are?"

"Alex...Alex Gordon." Alex hesitated, not knowing whether to inquire about his Guardian friend but he wondered if Daniel Jordan and his friend had been sent there. "Did you run across a Guardian or his girlfriend—Daniel Jordan or Lydia Cohen—during your time in Leavenworth?"

Sebastian's theory of life was that there were no coincidences. "Yes, Daniel was my cellmate. I saw his friend Lydia in the exercise area a few times."

Alex didn't know where to take the conversation. He liked Daniel and was surprised when he learned he'd given up the Youth Council, refusing to bow before the golden statue. "What is life like in Leavenworth?"

"Well, Daniel is young and strong so they put him on labor details, building crews and digging graves. He often came in at night soaked to the bone and dripping mud, exhausted, sometimes too exhausted to eat. The last time I saw him he looked like a ghost weighed down with guilt that he'd deprived his friend of this beautiful city."

Alex nodded. His ideas of the administration had changed from his first months in the City of Gold. The Golden City wasn't so golden. It was immoral, mean-spirited, and selfish, beautiful on the outside but rotting on the inside.

"I'm to escort you while you're here," Alex said. "Like to see the assignment?"

They finished their meal, Alex allowing Sebastian to take his time. After dining, Alex led him down the path toward the golden statue.

"Sebastian Cramer, isn't it?" the statue called.

Sebastian withdrew to a safer distance. Like Daniel the golden statue of the president emitted an aura of darkness. "How does it know who I am?" he asked Alex.

"It's programmed but it wouldn't have your identification recorded. So…I don't really know."

Sebastian entered the area of the statue again. "How do you know me?"

"You were arrested as a homeless person and sent to Leavenworth prison. You are here to work on my hard disc. A genius who developed chips for Intel, I believe."

"Yes. What do you think is wrong with you?"

"I need a new lithium chip. The one inserted burned up. Can you design something unique for me, Sebastian?"

Stunned, Alex listened to the discourse between the statue and Sebastian, surprised that Sebastian seemed unafraid of the mechanical wonder.

"If I can find the right materials, I might be able to design something for you. Not tonight, however. It will take time."

Alex led Sebastian back to his suite. "How can the statue talk to you like that?"

"Simple, it's alive."

The next day, Sebastian scheduled a meeting with the Prophet who seemed greatly disturbed about something.

"I don't have much time for you," said the Prophet turning his back to Sebastian.

"I need to know your expectations for the statue."

"I want him fixed."

"How does he 'know' things, Prophet. I don't think his computerized memory is providing him current information."

The Prophet turned around, casting a menacing look at Sebastian. "What are you saying?"

"I'm saying the statue appears to be alive; yet, it's made out of metal. I need to know its construction so I can invent an appropriate chip for its hard drive."

"You are very astute, prisoner, but let us just say I have endowed the statue with some of my own life force. Your job is only to get the mechanical movements of the statue functioning again. Make a list of what you need. A short list. I expect the correction to be accomplished in three or four days upon which you will most likely be returned to Leavenworth. Do you understand?"

Sebastian stood. "I do. I've prepared the list. If it's permissible, I will enjoy your pool and recreational facilities until you are ready for me."

Sebastian studied the blueprints he'd drawn of the golden statue. He wished there was some way to destroy it but that meant destroying himself. *Was he ready to die?* Could he set a timer to release destroying the hard drive after he returned to Leavenworth? What future did he have there?

After thinking it over for a few minutes, Sebastian designed a new hard drive and chip, one that would cause the mouth and extremities to have some motion. Did he wish to be the Prophet's hi-tech guru?

Destroy the golden image, Sebastian. It does much harm.

So the Lord was putting thoughts in his mind again. All right. He set a timer on the chip and hard drive to explode forty-eight hours after he returned to Leavenworth. Then he bowed his head in silent prayer. *Do you have other work for me, Lord?*

The tap on Sebastian's door signaled the arrival of Alex, his appointed Guardian. His appointment with the Prophet was at eight-thirty a.m. Dread filled Sebastian like the poison from a rattlesnake's bite. He smiled at the picture in his mind of the Prophet in a snakeskin slithering between the City of Gold and Leavenworth.

Today, the Prophet would size Sebastian up and determine whether to offer him a job as a technical consultant, or whether he would hand over the materials Sebastian needed to finish the adjustments he'd begun on the golden statue and return him to Leavenworth.

Sebastian entered the Prophet's office. Again, he felt a wave of evil crash over his body.

"Well, Sebastian, sit down. Let's have a little talk. Are you enjoying the City of Gold?"

"Yes, sir. It certainly is a wonder."

"The engineering designs please you?"

"The designer outdid himself."

The Prophet smiled. "The city was designed by Omega I and myself. Of course, in a city of such technology, projects need tweaking from time to time. I want you to think whether you would like to become a resident of the City — our technology consultant, so to speak." He watched for Sebastian's reaction to his proposal. "Of course, you must meet certain basic standards. I understand you gave up your job taking care of your wife who had cancer and missed the time allotted for taking the number to buy and sell, thus causing you to become homeless. Is that a fair summary of your situation?"

"Yes, it is."

"You then would need to take the number before signing on to becoming part of the City of Gold. Is that a problem?"

Sebastian hesitated. If he accepted this position, he would sign away his soul. "It is a tempting offer. May I weigh my decision for a day or two?"

Disgusted, the Prophet turned his back on Sebastian. "You may consider the offer until you finish the statue. I assume that project will end soon?"

Sebastian replied that it would.

"You are dismissed. You will not be offered this position again. If you decline, you will be sent back to Leavenworth to finish your life sentence—a rather grim ending for someone of your obvious technical knowledge, don't you think?"

As Sebastian stared into the eyes of the Prophet, he sensed a darkness like nothing he'd ever experienced.

He left the office, his mind warring between the two alternatives: staying on as technical advisor for the Prophet or returning to Leavenworth. There should be no choice. Any sane person would choose to live in the beautiful new capital but Sebastian viewed the City of Gold as beautiful on the surface but full of darkness and immorality. Could he compromise his resurrected faith by staying in the City of Comfort, City of Idols, the City of Darkness although the alternative probably meant starvation and certain death. *Help me, Lord. Give me the peace and strength to do the right thing.*

Leaving this world caused Sebastian no fear. The more he wrestled with the choices, the clearer his path emerged.

His thoughts were interrupted by Alex. "So did he offer you a job?"

"He did."

"You taking it?"

Sebastian studied the young Guardian. "If I don't, it will mean I'll finish my life in Leavenworth. A rather bad ending, huh, Alex?"

"You know we're not really free here either, Sebastian. It's like a beautiful prison."

"Ah, yes, but you do eat well and sleep in comfort."

"True."

Sebastian didn't want to confide in the Guardian but Alex surprised him with his statements about the City of Gold being a prison. He returned to the golden statue hoping to disconnect its mouth before it told him his thoughts.

Sebastian wrestled again with the two alternatives. He corrected the statue's hard drive but set it to overload after his return to Leavenworth which would cause a meltdown of the golden statue. *"You promised to be with me, Lord. I'll need your strength to say no.*

Sebastian finished his work. Tonight he'd enjoy prime rib and a baked potato—perhaps his last meal. In the morning he'd report to the Prophet with his answer. But first he'd watch the news, shower,and have a good night's sleep. Then que sera, sera.

Sebastian dressed slowly. The loneliness that surrounded his heart without Callie gave him courage to face whatever lie ahead. He made his way with Alex to the office of the Prophet.

The Prophet nodded Sebastian in, ending his conversation. "Well, have you made a decision?"

"I have, sir. I am thankful for the offer of a good life, but I must decline. I am a Christian and my answer is no. I cannot take the number. I will return to Leavenworth."

The Prophet's patience with this technical expert ended. He reached into his desk drawer and pulled out a Smith and Wesson.380. Satisfied with the startled expression on Sebastian's face, he fired a bullet straight into his heart.

"Perhaps you will not return to Leavenworth after all."

Chapter Twenty-nine

A nother nightmare! Daniel rolled over and back again, tired of interrupted sleep when he was so exhausted. He closed his eyes, hoping for the escape that came with sleep only to be awakened this time by a dream—a dream he remembered having before. In the dream, his grandparents called softly... "Follow the light, Daniel, follow the light."

What did the dream mean? He sat up, rubbed his eyes, and examined the cell. Something was different. He waited for his eyes to adjust to the darkness; then he examined the cell walls. A strange light hovered over the lock on the cell door.

Daniel forced himself from the cot. Slowly, he walked toward the light. It grew brighter the closer he got. His heart pounded. He reached out to touch the light. As his hands wrapped around the bars, the door swung open. Shaking, he walked through it and followed the light down the prison corridor past sleeping prisoners. At the end of the row of men's cells the light turned sharply, continuing along the corridor to the women's cells. Daniel followed closely, barely breathing until the light stopped. Two women curled in the fetal position lay in the cell. One was Lydia, the other Elizabeth.

"Lydia," he whispered. "Wake up." Lydia stretched and came over to the door of her cell.

"Daniel, how did you get here? Where are you going?"

"I don't know. I had a dream. In the dream my grandpa said 'Follow the light.' So…I followed the light here."

Elizabeth coughed, awaking to the voices. "What is it, Lydia? Are you all right? Is it the Guardian?"

"No, it's Daniel. He's following a strange light."

Elizabeth walked over to Daniel. "In the beginning was the light, and the light was with God and the light was God. Children, I think God is rescuing you. He did this before in the olden times going before Moses and the people like a light. They were to follow the light and the cloud and they would be safe from the enemy. Hurry now and go with Daniel."

"But I can't leave you, Elizabeth. You're not well."

"Go, child. I don't have long in this world and I'm not well enough to go with you." She put her arms around Lydia and kissed her. "You will be safe with God."

Breathless, the two entered the corridor, not knowing what to expect. *How had the cell door unlocked?* Daniel's mind filled with the soft yellow light that had protected him from the laser treatments. And he knew...just like Elizabeth said, God was with them. Grasping Lydia's hand, they made their way like ghosts down the passageway. "Follow the light, Lydia. It's God. He's the light."

As the light touched each gate, the iron bars slid back. The guards stared through them unseeing as the two young people made their way through the prison. Finally, they reached the exercise yard. Daniel stopped. Looking up he saw the Guardians on the walkway. He and Lydia would be easy targets in the open space. If the Guardians saw them, they would shoot to kill. Daniel still had a wound from the bullet that grazed him in the ankle. The light continued, waiting for them. They'd come too far to turn back. Daniel squeezed Lydia's hand, pulling her into the open space. As they stepped into the courtyard, the light surrounded them like a luminous cloud.

"The light is protecting us, Lydia. I don't think they can see us. Hurry, God is leading us out."

"I'm afraid, Daniel."

He tightened his grip on Lydia's hand. When they reached the outside gate, the light hovered over the small door next to the main gate. Again, the guards seemed unaware of their presence. Daniel lifted the heavy metal bar releasing the rusty gate and they passed through arriving outside the wall of the fort. Afraid to talk, they groped their way along the wall. *Was it a dream? Where were they?*

Daniel and Lydia crept along the prison wall toward the east. The pre-dawn fog and drizzle chilled them but they pushed forward desperate to put distance between them and the prison.

"I'm so cold, Danny."

"I know Lydia; try to keep moving." Daniel wondered how long it would be before they were discovered missing. The sun rose and then he saw it…the field where he'd dug graves. Unable to protect Lydia from the sight, Daniel stopped and put his arm around her. He felt sick thinking of all the terrible things they had been through.

"Oh, Daniel…it's the graves."

So many innocent people killed by this terrible government. Daniel bent down to read the marker of a new grave, then straightened up. "Keep going, Lydia."

"Who is it, Danny? Someone we know?" Lydia knelt down to read the marker. "The grave is empty but the marker says Sebastian Cramer. Oh, Danny... your cellmate." Tears came to her eyes.

Sickened by the thought of what the Prophet might have done with Sebastian, Daniel understood that his gut feeling was right. Sebastian was in terrible trouble, maybe dead already. *Sebastian, did they ask you to take the number? Did you cross the Prophet?* Either way Sebastian was a dead man. Daniel hated this brutal regime. He guessed Sebastian finally had enough. *Dear God, I hope he's with you.*

He took Lydia's arm, suddenly feeling God's presence no longer with them. *Where should they go? Why did you desert us, God?* Daniel heard a bark in the distance. *The dogs... please, God, don't let them find us. You know they'll kill us.*

Lydia and Daniel approached a vine-covered gazebo on the far side of the cemetery. Separating the vines, they squeezed inside. Stone benches lined the gazebo. Still sobbing softly, Lydia sank down, resting her head on the moss-covered wall. The shock of seeing the graves, and fearing that soon Elizabeth would be buried in one, opened the floodgates. She closed her eyes, and Daniel let her grieve for the woman who'd been like a mother to her. He didn't have the heart to force her on. Lydia buried her head on his chest.

Daniel's eyes were heavy. He leaned back on the stone wall fighting to stay awake. A crackling sound jolted him awake. Someone was walking in the leaves outside the gazebo. Hearing a twig snap, he touched Lydia lightly signally her not to talk. They held their breath.

Out of the morning fog, two figures armed with rifles headed straight for the gazebo. Helpless without a weapon, Daniel grabbed a fallen branch. The two figures coming toward them wore masks and camouflage clothing. They didn't look like guards from the prison and they didn't have dogs with them. Who were these men? What business did they have in such a remote place?

Chapter Thirty

A t night, the patrol from Liberty Farm made their rounds. Armed and dressed in camouflage, they watched Leavenworth and the City of Gold from the deserted gazebo. In the cemetery nearby, they discovered twenty-five newly-filled graves. Whatever was happening at the prison had begun. They would take their lookout in the gazebo and leave shortly before dawn. The patrol leader signaled the patrol to stop. The sound of barking dogs meant trouble. He searched the gazebo with his eyes making out two figures. Could it be escapees from the prison?

Daniel clutched the branch, ready to defend Lydia. Disappointment flooded his body.

The leader of the scouting group laid down his rifle and climbed into the gazebo, warning Lydia and Daniel not to talk. "We're friends. Don't make any noise. Follow us."

A short distance later, the leader spoke into his walkie-talkie… "Bill, I think we discovered our missing couple. Tell Martha to put on the grub."

A large white farmhouse appeared before them, its paint peeling. Smoke curled from the chimney and chickens darted across the front porch. The smell of bacon hung in the air. Daniel blinked back exhausted tears of relief. Then he saw it…a black motorcycle. *His Black Mustang?*

Daniel ran his hand along the sides of the machine. He turned to Lydia who looked puzzled. "It's my motorcycle, Lydia. My dad must have been here." *How did he know to bring it here?* Daniel unbuckled one of the saddlebags. Inside he found his leather cowboy boots and a note:

"Danny, I've left your cycle with the people of Liberty Farm. They are to use it with the promise that they'll search for you in the event you escape the City of Gold. We love you, Daniel. May the God of the universe watch over you, Dad."

In the other saddlebag Daniel discovered Grandpa's small wooden box wrapped in his favorite flannel shirt with a pair of Levis. He opened the box and unfolded the map, unable to believe that they were standing in front of one of the "R's" shown on the map.

Lydia gasped. "Is it a real Bible?"

Daniel nodded. "My grandpa's. You can read the stories of Jesus for yourself now." He handed the precious Book to Lydia.

Overcome with fatigue and stress, Lydia whispered, "The Lord *is* watching over us, Danny."

The young couple walked toward the big man coming out of the farmhouse.

"As you can see, your dad was here a few weeks ago. He asked us to be on the lookout for you, but we never dreamed you could escape Leavenworth, if in fact, you were there."

"It's a long story…"

"First things, first. You look starved. How would you like an old-fashioned breakfast?"

The kitchen smelled of cider and cinnamon. Lydia and Daniel exchanged glances. *Was this real? Were they actually going to have a home-cooked breakfast?*

"After you eat, maybe you can tell us a little about your adventures."

"We'd be happy to, sir."

"Bill, just call me Bill."

Daniel and Lydia ate as though they were starving and, in truth, they were. The warmth of the stove filled the room and the two wilted, overcome with fatigue.

"Kids, let's take a rain check on that talk. You both need a hot bath and bed. Martha will take good care of you." Bill noticed the boy's head had been shaved, he wore a beard and baggy light blue scrubs. But it was the girl who broke his heart. Her hair had been chopped off, and she was as thin as a ghost.

Martha sensed the young couple needed some pampering. "Daniel, I've been heating some water for a nice hot bath. Would you like this shaving gear?" She laid out the supplies, adding a thick towel to the pile. Then she noticed the dried blood on Daniel's scrubs. She looked up at him. "They shot you?" Without waiting for an answer, she reached in the drawer and pulled out scissors with which she cut the pant leg. "It looks like a surface wound. The bullet didn't go in?"

"No, just tore off surface skin and muscle. I washed it up and it seems to be healing. It'll be good to soak it in a bath."

Martha nodded, satisfied that Daniel's leg was all right. She'd bandage it when he finished. Then turning to Lydia, she said, "I'll spoil Lydia a little and then you two can hit the sack for a few hours." She motioned Lydia to follow her. "I used to be a beautician in my other life," she winked. "Could I offer you a shampoo and haircut?"

Lydia stood paralyzed. *How could this farm woman know what she needed?* "I'd like that, Martha."

Martha began to style Lydia's hair. "You have beautiful hair. It'll soon grow out, but we'll help it a little." After the cut, Martha ran another bath adding some fragrant bath salts. She placed a clean nightgown by the tub. "You'll find a bed in the next room when you're finished."

Lydia nodded. The warm water lifted away the ache in her heart. She closed her eyes wanting the moment to last forever. After she toweled off, she put on the flannel nightgown and fell into the old-fashioned featherbed.

Meanwhile Martha searched the clothes closet for something to fit Lydia. Poor girl—skin and bones. Lydia's hair made Martha's eyes water, if only people knew how cruel this regime really was. She chose some underclothes, a pair of jeans, sweatshirt, and a sheepskin jacket with a scarf, putting them on a chair next to Lydia's bed. She'd ask Lydia what size shoe she wore when she woke up.

Bill finished cleaning the kitchen. His mind explored the possibilities for Daniel and Lydia. At last, he made his decision. He signaled the farmhands for a meeting. "I think we have a few hours. As soon as Daniel and Lydia are missed, the guards will begin an area search."

"The dogs were already barking, Bill."

"Normally, I wouldn't be concerned. We're a working farm. But the motorcycle is a dead giveaway. Darryl, could you drive it out to the hills and hide it in the brush? They need sleep. We'll buy them some time. Now hurry."

Towards evening the smell of fried chicken and corn on the cob woke the pair who dressed and met in the hall. They sat down at the long plank table, joining the people of Liberty Farm. Everyone held hands while Bill prayed: *"Lord, you are our shield and deliverer. Thank you for the rescue of these two young people. We pray your protection over them and a place of safety. Bless this food to our bodies' use. Amen."*

Bill waited until everyone finished dinner, then he said, "Daniel, your dad hoped that you and Lydia were still alive. He brought your motorcycle so you'd have a way to escape."

"But how did he know where to bring it?" Daniel interrupted.

"He's a smart man. Dr. Hart's nurse talked to her pastor who gave your dad a map of our safe houses."

"You mean like Rancho Christo?"

"Exactly. Your dad just picked the closest one to the City of Gold."

Daniel was amazed. Good ol' Dad. "What do you think we should do now, Bill?"

Bill frowned. He weighed Daniel and Lydia's options. They were so tired and rundown, he'd like to give them more rest and food, but an intuitive feeling made him say, "I think you need to leave as soon as possible."

One of the farmhands burst through the door. "Bill, they're on their way."

Martha signaled the kids to follow her. She led them quickly and quietly to a stone fruit cellar under the house. "Be very quiet..." She locked the door and left. Daniel put his arms around Lydia to stop her shaking. "It's all right."

Daniel's words melted the fear in Lydia's heart. A strange calm descended on her causing a tingle from head to toe. "He's here with us, Daniel. I can feel His Spirit."

Daniel also felt the calm.

They waited quietly in the back of the cold cellar. Canned peaches, cherries, beans, tomatoes, and corn formed rows on the shelves. Onions, potatoes, and apples filled bags stacked against the wall, and smoked hams, chickens and turkeys hung from the rafters. The fragrance was a potpourri of wonderful smells. Many minutes went by before the door opened and Martha shone a flashlight into the darkness. "It's all right; they're gone."

"Were they looking for us?"

"I'm sure they were, but we're a working farm and that's what they found."

Bill waited in the kitchen with a sober look on his face. "You aren't safe here."

He unfolded the map pointing to the safe house in Canada. "This is the only place you'll be safe. It's the city of refuge for all Christians who can't take the number. Our government has no authority in Canada. You'll be safe there."

"Is this where the remnant is gathering?" Daniel asked.

So this young man knew about the remnant. "Many exiles have made it to our safe house in Canada where they wait for Jesus' return. The village provides a school, a health center, food, cabins, and a lodge. You and Lydia will find you are needed there.

"The people study the teachings of Jesus; you can learn a lot. I think you are safe to spend one more night, but first, we'd like to hear how you and Lydia escaped from Leavenworth."

The group moved over by the fireplace where Daniel and Lydia told them about life in Leavenworth and their unbelievable escape.

"Tell us about the prisoners. Who are they?" asked Bill.

"Good honest people: reporters, ministers, media, lawyers, and people who did not take the number," replied Daniel.

"My best friend was an older Christian lady who tried to keep people from taking the number. A neighbor reported her before she found a safe place," said Lydia.

"The sad fact is they can't release the people from prison. They don't want dissidents stirring up resistance to the government," Daniel said.

"Could this new initiative to allow lifers to give their organs be related to that?"

"Of course. As they arrest more and more people, they have to find a way to get rid of them."

"The graves?"

"Organ donors."

"Diabolical."

The next morning Bill, Lydia, Daniel, and two members of Bill's patrol climbed into the hills to pick up the Honda. Darryl led the way, clearing pine boughs he'd used to camouflage the cave. Daniel checked the gear. Besides packing beef jerky, apples, and a loaf of freshly baked bread, Martha sent a lunch. Daniel tied on some bedrolls and Bill handed him the gas card left by his father.

"It still has about a hundred dollars on it, Daniel. Be careful and remember the stations have security cameras. Don't pull into them unless you have to. Put these safety goggles on. They contain a polymer that makes iris identification difficult. And...remember, we'll be praying for you. Good luck, kids."

Daniel helped Lydia onto the motorcycle, then pressed the accelerator causing the motorcycle to roar. "You up for this, Lydia?"

"I'm right behind you," Lydia joked, "and I'm sure not letting go."

They waved goodbye to their benefactors and, following Bill's advice, chose a small scenic road to avoid the interstates. *Were they free at last?* Lydia hoped so. She never wanted to go back to Leavenworth...never. She would rather die first.

Chapter Thirty-one

Rage burned in the heart of the Prophet. Dr. Hart did not report to Leavenworth for his end of the world transportation via Jerry. Seething, he tried to contact Jerry. Had something happened to the old plane or was Jerry a traitor? For the first time in his relationship with the old pilot, he received no answer to his communication. Frustrated, the Prophet wrote himself a memo to send a Guardian for Jerry's mother. There was more than one way to handle this.

A bigger problem loomed. How could anyone escape from Leavenworth? Why hadn't the guards noticed the young couple? The Prophet set his jaw. His eyes burned with an unholy fire. He pounded his fist on the desk. Someone would pay. He buzzed Omega I.

"Good news? Dr. Hart had a change of mind?" said the president.

"Dr. Hart entered the helicopter, but did not arrive at Leavenworth. Uncooperative, he chose to end his life as an organ donor rather than serve his country as its organ donor doctor. I fear our pilot rescued him and deserted us. I'm handling it. This, however, is not the problem of the moment. The two young Youth Council members escaped last night."

"I thought Leavenworth was escape-proof."

The Prophet stroked his beard. "I'm looking into it. I'll execute one Guardian and one prisoner. I don't want any new attempts to escape. It had to be a Guardian."

"Weren't the Guardians handpicked for duty?"

"Yes, but then so were Jordan and Cohen. Humans often disappoint."

The Prophet pulled up each Guardian's file studying his background. Finally, Rick Hathaway appeared on his monitor. Hathaway was one of the Prophet's favorites. He had plans for him, but as he scanned the dossier, he saw that Rick had been partnered with Daniel Jordan as a Guardian. Was that it? Did Rick help Daniel and Lydia escape? He spoke into his communicator. "Bring Rick Hathaway to my office."

"Yes sir, right away."

The Prophet stared out his window at the city he and the president had created...a masterpiece. While he waited, he formulated a plan.

Rick followed the older Guardian to the helicopter. The Prophet wanted to see him. Hope rose like the foam on a beer. The Prophet knew his name. Perhaps he was being promoted. The aircraft landed and the escort signaled him to follow. He'd never seen the City of Gold. Awed at the blue glass buildings and the underground river running under the sidewalks, he longed to leave Leavenworth and be part of this magical city.

Arriving at the Prophet's office, Rick took a seat in the waiting room. A half hour went by. He tried to kid the secretary, but she was stern and unfriendly. The atmosphere seemed ominous. A chill ran down his spine. *He* was *here for a promotion, wasn't he?*

The Prophet turned to face Rick. "Sit down."

Rick obeyed. He was getting nervous.

The Prophet opened a file. "You did well in your training as a Guardian?"

"Yes, sir." *Maybe it was going to go better than he thought.*

"You were assigned to the Center for New Age Medicine?"

"Yes, sir."

"Daniel Jordan was your partner?"

"Yes, sir." Rick began to sweat. *Where was this going?*

"Was Daniel a good partner?"

"He was okay."

"You're happy with your work at Leavenworth?"

"Yes, sir, I am…but I hope someday to be assigned here in the City of Gold."

The Prophet raised his eyebrows. "Did you know Daniel was a prisoner at Leavenworth?"

Rick closed his eyes. "Yes, I saw him."

"He escaped with a girl last night. Would you know anything about that?"

Rick's heart stopped. *Did the Prophet think he'd helped Daniel escape?* "No, sir, I don't. But how could anyone escape Leavenworth?"

"My thought, exactly. They would have to have help. Someone on the inside, right, Rick?"

Rick's dreams crashed. He'd be lucky to get out of here alive. The Prophet was angry, and circumstantial evidence pointed to Rick.

The Prophet turned, "Put him in the hold. Perhaps he'll feel like talking in a few days."

The Guardian MP shoved Rick out of the office, then put handcuffs on him. In one brief session, Rick's future lie shattered on the floor of the Prophet's office.

Chapter Thirty-two

"We have the rat in the maze," said the Prophet.

"An interesting game. What do you expect to happen?" the president asked.

"Well, he'll either lead us to the two young dissidents or..."

"What if he's innocent?"

"That would make the game infinitely more interesting. We will discover what makes Rick Hathaway tick."

Seven days in solitary, unable to stand up or shower, wore Rick down. And the darkness was getting on his nerves. He disciplined himself to eat whatever was shoved in the small door to the cell whether it was putrid grass soup with slime floating in it or tasteless gruel.

No more interrogations…no beatings…no one to talk to—that was getting on his nerves, too. *How long would they keep him in solitary?*

He spent hours trying to understand how Daniel and the girl escaped. *Who helped them?* There was simply no way out of Leavenworth without someone's help. He wasn't angry with Daniel but one and one added up to two to the Prophet. However, in Rick's case, one and one didn't make two.

Rick watched the rat that shared the hole with him. Every day he gave it a crumb of bread. Each time the rat ran into the corner, scratched the dirt, and buried it. How long could it live without food? Maybe he shouldn't waste his bread.

On the flight from the City of Gold, the Guardian MP told Rick two people would be executed to reinforce security, a prisoner and a guard. *Was he to be executed to teach the guards a lesson?* It made sense in an evil sort of way. But he was only twenty-one years old. He dropped into position and did fifty pushups—punishment for letting his mind wander.

Ray Jones, a Fox journalist before the president closed down the news channel, criticized the president's initiatives, especially the Ascension, saying it was a waste of taxpayer money. Presenting an alternative point of view, Ray offered the idea of limiting health services to old people when they reached a certain age but then letting them die naturally. No need to make a spectacle out of helpless people. It soured citizens against the new government. He even challenged the government to rethink their policy, offering to serve on a national committee to solve the health care dilemma. Washington issued a flight for Ray and flew him directly to Leavenworth—so much for free speech.

The Prophet wanted to make a statement no prisoner would ever forget. He chose the young Fox journalist to be the star of the show. He set the date for his execution the following day, sending a message to all networks and to the prisoners in Leavenworth. The doctor they called the Boston Butcher, hired to do organ removal, would put him out of his misery. No precedent for escape would be allowed. Justice demanded an example. What better way to silence Jones and end the hope of prisoners than a hanging.

The buzz around the prison said two inmates escaped. An impossible feat. Everyone was on edge. What would happen to the inmates if someone actually got out of Leavenworth? A deadly silence fell on the prison, broken only by the sound of barking dogs. A time bomb of anxiety lurked in every cell.

Not surprised when a few nights later the Guardians prodded them into the barren gymnasium, the prisoners were startled to see a temporary scaffold set up. Was someone to be executed? The prisoners took their seats on the rusty chairs provided. The atmosphere in the room was deathly quiet. Fear permeated the air like a black funnel cloud. Some of the women wept...the men stared at the floor. Then the Boston Butcher appeared, leading a young man to the scaffold. The doctor walked slowly to the microphone but as he began to talk, low singing filled the room.

Were you there when they crucified my Lord?

Were you there when they crucified my Lord?

Oh!...Sometimes it causes me to tremble, tremble, tremble.

Were you there when they crucified my Lord?

A hush fell as the young man, a journalist, was marched to the gallows. He stared ahead as the singing resumed. As the rope tightened around his neck, lifting him into the air, the government flexed its muscle, deed done. The prisoners understood the message and made their way back to their cells.

Rick listened to the weird singing, not knowing where it came from. *Were they executing the prisoner tonight?* Earlier, the guard told Rick he would also be executed on the following night. It wasn't fair. Why were they wasting such talent when he could be of so much use to the Prophet? He wanted desperately to tell the Prophet that he'd do anything, to be part of this government.

He contemplated the rat who now lay exhausted in the corner dying. *Why hadn't he tried to survive?* Rick kicked dirt on the rat's body. He was not like the rat. Give him a chance. He'd prove he wasn't a traitor. One and one did not make two. He had hopes, aspirations...what about the money they'd invested in his training? He was good! He didn't deserve to die like the rat. He wanted to live.

Food shoved into the hole broke his attention. He surveyed the sandwich, not caring what was inside, finally biting into the dried, moldy bread. His teeth hit metal. He heaved a sigh of relief. Someone was giving him a chance to escape. He slid the electronic key into the door. Amazingly, it opened but Rick stayed in his cell waiting for night. He was familiar with the entire layout of the prison. After midnight, with fewer guards on duty, he would slip out of the cell and through the maze of corridors. His only plan—to survive. Capture meant instant death.

Later that night, he snaked his way down the dark passageways staying close to the walls and avoiding light. Using his instincts as a bat uses radar, he listened for the sound of voices. If he timed things right, he might be able to get past the guards and out of the prison. He was glad the solitary cells were near the exit.

At last, Rick reached the small side gate that led to the back of the prison. Trained to watch for prisoners, he now searched the yards for guards. At three a.m. the guards changed, providing Rick the best chance for escape. While they checked the books, Rick moved into the shadows, slipping the key into the rusty gate lock. The gate groaned but swung open. He was free at last.

The night air slapped Rick in the face as he ran in the direction of the trees. Breathless, he found himself standing next to the open graves dug for the organ donors. Where could he go? He searched the area spotting an old gazebo half-hidden in the woods. He'd rest for a few minutes and make a plan. A week in solitary had taken its toll.

The Prophet never slept. He watched the monitor, admiring Rick's stealth as he made his way out of the prison. Rick would be his bait. The Prophet would soon know if Rick helped the young couple escape. The electronic passkey in his pocket would beam Rick's whereabouts to their guidance system. The game was on...

Chapter Thirty-three

The patrol from Liberty Farm crept through the woods surrounding the Leavenworth cemetery. The number of graves increased each day, making the cemetery appear like a granite garden. After hearing Daniel's escape story, the men on the patrol doubted there would be more escapes. For whatever reason, God intervened on behalf of the young couple.

As the patrol neared the gazebo where they spent their night watch on the prison, they spied a form barely identifiable lying on a bench. They surrounded the man, noting his battered uniform. *Was he the enemy or another fugitive?* The patrol leader picked up his communicator. "Bill, there's a bearded man in a beat-up uniform in the gazebo."

"Keep me posted, don't take chances."

"Roger that."

The sound of voices broke through Rick's deep sleep. He waited, heart pumping with hope that it wasn't the guards from the prison. "Don't shoot. I'm unarmed." Rick got to his feet unsure whether the men were a search party from Leavenworth or townspeople. "Who are you?"

"I think the better question is, who are you, son? Are you lost or have you run away?"

Rick hesitated. "A little of both, I guess. There was a misunderstanding and…" His voice drifted off.

"You look tired, boy. When was your last good meal? Why don't you come back to our farm. You can fill us in there."

Rick followed the men still unsure of who they were, his guess — probably townspeople. But why did they wear camouflage and have guns? If he could get a meal or two, some civilian clothes, and a good night's sleep, he'd buy some time and be able to formulate a plan. He was far too visible in his Guardian uniform.

"What's the uniform?" one of the men asked.

"I was a Guardian stationed at Leavenworth."

So this kid *was* the enemy. Good thing Daniel and the girl had left. The patrol leader would warn Bill and Martha.

A dilapidated old farmhouse came into view. A heavy-set man in overalls walked out to meet them.

"Name's Bill. You look like you could stand a good meal." Bill patted Rick on the shoulder as Rick withdrew from the farmer's touch.

"I could. A cup of coffee would be great."

"My wife will take good care of you, son. Martha's the best cook in the area."

Rick surveyed the farm. When he entered the kitchen and saw a wood-fed stove and hand water pump, he knew the people must be from the old ways. The farm was a place for people who wouldn't take the number and a diabolical plan entered his mind.

Bill pulled the old-fashioned coffeepot off the stove and poured a steaming mug of coffee for the shivering young man. "Tell me about yourself while we wait for Martha."

"Name's Rick Hathaway. I was a Guardian stationed at Leavenworth but there was a misunderstanding and…"

"What kind of misunderstanding?" Bill asked.

"This guy escaped from Leavenworth. We both were Guardians in Phoenix. I guess the Prophet thought I helped him escape."

"Did you?"

"No, I didn't even know he'd escaped."

Bill's mind was working overtime. *Could this be a ruse to smoke out Daniel and Lydia?* The Guardian uniform disturbed him. This man was the enemy. They would feed and rest him but then, send him on his way as soon as possible. Under no circumstances would Bill reveal that Daniel and Lydia had been guests also. "You enjoy your coffee, Rick."

Bill signaled Martha and the boys to join him. "My gut tells me to be careful," he said in a low voice. "Don't mention the young couple being here. This could be a setup to learn where they are." Bill returned to Rick.

"Did you see a guy about my age?" Rick asked.

"Not recently, son. How long ago did he escape?"

"About a week ago, I guess. Maybe I could join him if I could find him." Rick waited to see if Bill bought this.

Bill shook his head. "Sorry, can't help you. Give you some clean clothes though, if you're interested."

Wolfing down his food, Rick nodded. After he finished eating, Bill ushered Rick into a bedroom straight from the 1800s, quilt and all. He dug in some drawers pulling out jeans and a flannel jacket. "Here, put these on; they should fit. If you want, we can heat some water for a bath."

It was amazing to Rick how these people lived without any electronics or up-to-date appliances and systems. He'd seen horses corralled and cattle in the distance plus a few chickens. *Could they survive without being part of the government? If so, why hadn't their neighbors reported them?* They were definitely dissidents.

Rick bathed and changed into the jeans and flannel shirt. He checked out the room. A small book sat on top of the doily-covered lamp table. Rick opened the cover. The Bible. Then he saw them, light blue scrubs shoved under the bed. So…Daniel had been here. *Who were these people? Why did they lie to him about Daniel?* If he were still a guard, he would interrogate all of them and do whatever it took to make them talk. They had no right aiding and abetting criminals — himself excluded.

These people not only helped Daniel, they evidently followed the old ways keeping the forbidden book. Rick left the bedroom. He thought about all the people of the old ways in Leavenworth — the graves they filled. Somehow, he would use these farm people to regain the Prophet's favor. Through the lace-curtained bedroom window he noticed Bill climb into a truck. Uncomfortable, Rick wanted to leave. He leaped off the porch waving at Bill to stop. He'd get a motel in town.

"Can I catch a ride into town?"

"Hop in."

Rick climbed into the old Ford truck next to Bill. *How did he get gas?* As they rode in silence, Rick's plan to regain the Prophet's favor began to take shape. Lucky for him he still had the laser number to buy and sell. After he got a motel room, he'd get his supplies and contact the City of Gold. He'd show the Prophet that Rick Hathaway was material for his special forces.

Martha placed the last breakfast dish in the cupboard. The nagging fear started yesterday. *What did it mean? Is it you, Lord?*

"Something on your mind, dear?" Bill asked, noting Martha's frown.

"A nagging, upsetting feeling started yesterday. I don't know what it is."

"Have you had it before?"

"Only once, just before I went to the hospital for gall bladder surgery."

"The time you fell?"

"Exactly. Just before I went in I had this panicky fear like I was in danger. I didn't know what it was or what to do so I just prayed about it...asked God to protect me and keep me safe."

"And it's the same feeling?"

"Yes it is. Exactly the same."

"What does it make you want to do, Martha?"

Martha stopped and thought. "I think it makes me want to leave the farm — go away."

Bill nodded. Martha put his feeling into words. Something terrible was about to happen. "Let's make a plan. We'll get the camper ready. You take care of the food and clothes while I fill up some extra gas and check the oil. I'll tell the boys to take off for a couple of days."

"What about the animals?" Martha asked.

"We'll take Punch. I'll put feed and water for the other animals. They'll have to survive till we get back."

The couple had learned not to question the moving of the Spirit of God in their hearts. Martha stocked the camper, adding their small Bible and a few other precious mementos. It was better not to hold on to house and things too tightly.

"All set?"

"Yes, I think so." She took a last look at the little farm that sheltered so many. Grieving, she reached over and ruffled Punch's snowy ears. Petting the little black and white dog comforted her. *Would they return?* "Goodbye, Liberty Farm," she whispered.

Rick rented a rundown truck from the local garage, thankful he'd gotten the number tattooed on his hand which enabled him to buy what he needed. He picked up a rifle and supplies from the Liberty hardware store, but no store in the little burg carried communicators. Frustrated, Rick asked the druggist how they did email.

"Oh, those who want to send email go into the city and buy a communicator. Not much need for one here in the country. You can always go to the library and use their old computer."

Rick thanked the druggist for the information, and asked for directions to the library, hoping his plan still worked. Entering the building, a thin, elderly woman greeted him. Putting on his best manners, Rick asked if there was a computer he could use. The librarian frowned.

"It's locked up in that small study room," she said. "Do you have a library card?"

"No, Ma'am, but this is an emergency. Can't you make an exception?"

The librarian studied Rick, looking him up and down. "Not supposed to...but...maybe just this once." She took a key from a drawer in front of her and signaled Rick to follow her.

Rick breathed a sigh of relief. He didn't want attention or trouble before he completed his mission. "How do I turn on your computer?"

The librarian blushed. "The password is Hattie62... Hattie is my name."

He thanked the librarian, closed the door, and booted up the computer. He'd memorized the Prophet's private email, making it possible to contact him.

Remembering his short stay in Leavenworth, Rick shuddered. How did one blackmail someone as important as the Prophet? Perhaps blackmail wasn't the right word. How did one trade information and perform a duty in exchange for favors?

Should Rick contact the Prophet before or after he finished his plan? The Prophet was insulated by security. Did he check his own email? Rick doubted it. He probably let his secretary forward important messages. How should Rick word a note to get the Prophet's attention? He typed.

Prophet@CityofGold: *Prophet...Discovered Christian underground safe house used by Daniel Jordan and girl... Liberty, Kansas. Farmhouse used to aid dissidents. Watch for fireworks. Incinerator@liberty.* He pressed Send. *Did the Prophet leave the key for him to get out because he thought Rick would lead him to Daniel?* This was Rick's last chance to get reinstated. Satisfied that the email might gain the Prophet's attention, he returned the room key to the old woman.

"Thanks, Hattie, you're a lifesaver." Then Rick had a terrible thought. How would he send a video of the mission without his communicator? "Hattie, do you have a video camera I could rent?"

"No, but the druggist sells cameras. He may be able to help you."

The project kept falling apart. Without a video of his adventure, Rick would have no power with the Prophet. He returned to the drugstore and was able to purchase a disposable, digital, video camera. Old, but hopefully still workable.

Rick jumped into the truck and double-checked his supplies: explosives, gasoline, sleeping bag, water, grub.

Silently, he drove back to the motel where he planned to get a few hours sleep before going out to the old farmhouse.

About dusk, Rick awoke, grabbed a jacket, and set out for the farm. When he arrived, the horses were grazing in the fenced lot next to the barn. No sign of life, but it was supper time and his plan would take place after nine p.m. when all the hands were in bed. Till then, Rick would wait. He was pleased to see smoke curling out of the chimney.

After dark, Rick crawled down the incline behind the farmhouse. He placed the explosives under the porch not really caring about the people inside, his only focus—to get back in the good graces of the Prophet. Too bad about the old farm lady, she was a pretty good cook. He set the timer and returned to the hill to watch the fireworks.

Taking the outdated disposable video camera, he prepared to video the explosion so that he could send a movie showing the destruction. He checked his watch...three minutes. For Rick it was the longest three minutes in his lifetime. The explosion blew out the glass windows and ignited the gasoline. He waited for the people to come running out of the house, but realized they might have been killed in the explosion. The flames licked at the old farmhouse and spread to the barns. An icy excitement thrilled him. Loading his rifle, he aimed at the animals. He had a soft spot for dumb animals. He would shoot them before the fire reached them.

Rick took the camera, purchased a mailer, and dropped it in the mail. The next morning he returned to the library, flirted with Hattie, and settled down to send an email to the Prophet. He hoped the Prophet was a dealmaker.

Prophet@CityofGold. *In reference to film, Liberty Farm destroyed. No sign of Daniel Jordan but know he has been here with girl. Found prison garb in house on earlier visit. Hoping to be reinstated as Guardian in City of Gold. My loyalty is with you. Reply. Incinerator@Liberty. Thanks for the key.*

The Prophet's plan worked well. Rick was his. Had he murdered all the people at Liberty Farm trying to prove his loyalty? Maybe he was worth salvaging. The Prophet had plenty of extermination to do with the ever-growing number of dissidents.

It was unfortunate that Lydia and Daniel escaped. The Prophet needed to make an example of them for the others at Leavenworth. He wanted no more attempts to escape. Sending a signal to all security centers, he raised their capture to the highest priority. Electronically speaking, it was a small world and they couldn't get far without being detected, especially without the number which the Prophet's records showed they didn't have. He made a note to himself to monitor their parents' homes carefully in case they ventured to contact them. Omega I wanted no loose ends. He sent Rick a safe signal: Incinerator@Liberty. *The Prophet says come home.*

For the third time Rick entered the library. Hattie immediately unlocked the study unaware she was aiding and abetting a criminal. He checked the email. Finally, a message appeared...*Come home.*

And come home he would, but first he returned to Liberty Farm to make a final check. He pushed the truck, not caring about speed. The Prophet wanted him to come home. When he reached the hill overlooking the farmhouse, he shut off the truck's engine and climbed the hill. The animals lay dead. The farm was smoking charcoal. Job finished.

Tears ran down Martha's face.

"What is it, Martha?" asked Bill.

"We don't need to go back; it's too late."

"What do you mean?"

"I mean whatever happened is over and there is no reason to go back."

"But Martha."

"I know, Bill, I know. We must go on to another safe house."

"Don't you think we should find out what happened?"

"I think it's too dangerous now. We have no way to let the other safe houses know unless we can get to a new one. What is nearest? Minnesota?"

Bill pondered Martha's words. He needed closure. "I'm going back, Martha. I need to."

Martha sighed. It was no good trying to talk Bill out of going back. His mind was set in cement. Bill started the engine and they drove two hours to the farm. The sky was blackened with smoke from the burning farm. As they got closer, Bill saw the animals lying on the ground in a pool of blood. Someone had shot them, all of them. Martha was right; the farm was gone. He turned away and squeezed Martha's hand. "I'm sorry, honey."

"God is good. He told us, Bill."

Chapter Thirty-four

S cottsdale: Eleven p.m. Harry's communicator vibrated in his pocket. He flipped it open.

"Mr. Jordan?"

"Yes."

"Pastor Neal here. Coffee six a.m.?"

"I'll be there." Harry hung up the phone aware that Judith was listening.

"Who was calling so late?" she asked.

Harry hesitated, not knowing how much to reveal. He didn't want to stir things up by mentioning Daniel's name. He and his wife's relationship was better, but still fragile.

"Nothing important." He busied himself tuning in the eleven o'clock news.

The voice of the president was saying, "Iran claims credit for the nuclear explosion in DC." He hesitated, then continued. "We believe Iran was flexing its nuclear muscle to warn the world—and especially America—that they will tolerate no interference in the Middle East from America.

"Because of world concern, I've been asked to head up the World Federation. I will still remain your president."

Judith frowned. "Harry, do you think there'll be more attacks?"

"Probably. They may try to hit New York again, maybe Los Angeles."

"Phoenix?"

"Anywhere, Judith, if they want to kill people and frighten us. Phoenix isn't a financial center but during bowl games, a lot of people come into the city."

"I hoped the One World Religion would stop all these religious wars. I always felt safe from war here in the U.S."

"The coastal cities are vulnerable to nuclear attack. That's probably one reason the government moved to the City of Gold. The military can protect the president and his officials better inland."

Afraid of waking Judith, Harry dressed and left the house. He started the engine on the SUV, irritated that he couldn't replenish the gas. Judith pushed him constantly to take the mark but the deadline was over; Harry was now a dissident.

Traffic was moderate and Harry arrived at the apartment a few minutes early. He tapped on the apartment door. Pastor Neal greeted him warmly, ushering him into his kitchen where they filled a couple of mugs with coffee."

"I've some news about Daniel. I received an astonishing email from Liberty Farm. The scouts picked up Daniel and Lydia. Bill said the two escaped Leavenworth prison through a miracle. They helped the kids, gave them false IDs, clothes, and provisions and sent them to Canada. We can only hope they make it through the border security—a very dangerous trip. I thought you'd want to know."

Harry tried to digest the news...Daniel was alive. He was thankful he'd followed his hunch about the motorcycle. Relief swept over him.

"So they put Daniel in Leavenworth."

"Yes, your son told them that many Christian dissidents, reporters, and human rights activists were captive in Leavenworth…and they are killing inmates in the organ donor program."

"I was afraid of that."

"Your son was very blessed to get out when he did."

"But how?"

"I wish I could tell you, but Bill didn't send that information. Should you keep this from your wife?"

Harry put his head in his hands. "I wouldn't if I thought she'd be glad. But I don't trust her since she got the number… and if Daniel is trying to get into Canada, she's better not knowing he's escaped. At least she can't betray him again." Harry took a long sip of coffee.

"Did you see the news?" asked Pastor Neal.

"You mean the president's announcement that Iran blew up DC? I don't understand why the Muslims hate us so much."

"I'm not sure it was Iran."

Harry looked puzzled. "Then who?"

"The Christian blog suspects Omega I and the Prophet."

Harry was flabbergasted. "They would detonate a nuclear bomb killing our own people? Surely you're not serious."

"I'm deadly serious. This president has hidden motives. It creates world sympathy. By destroying all symbols of freedom, it leaves nothing but his City of Gold."

"I saw the city from a distance, miles under some kind of shield."

Pastor Neal raised his eyebrows, "It's a counterfeit of the New Jerusalem, the biblical city of God."

Harry tried to absorb the pastor's statement. "You mean my father was right. The president could be the Antichrist?"

"It's possible. The World Federation asked him to be president. He'll control the world economically, religiously, and in all ways. Did you take the number to buy and sell?"

"No, Judith pressured me, but no...I didn't take the number."

The pastor clasped Harry's hands. "You did the right thing, Harry. Taking the number makes you belong to the powers of darkness. Something happens, and the people are deceived about many things."

Harry nodded. Perhaps that explained why Judith saw only the administration's point of view and why she considered Daniel the enemy. "I'm a dissident."

"Yes, you belong to a select few."

"I don't know how to run my business and take care of my family."

"It will be hard. I'm trying to decide whether to stay with my little group of believers here or flee to Rancho Christo to help Nan. I have to leave this apartment this week. The lease runs out."

Harry realized Neal also had a difficult decision. If he stayed, he would be able to encourage his people but would probably end up in prison.

He got up and shook hands with the pastor. "May God watch over you, sir. And...thank you for taking time to update me on Daniel."

"I'll keep them in my prayers."

"Thank you."

Chapter Thirty-five

The Prophet reviewed the video sent by Rick Hathaway, his new prodigy. The young Guardian had skills. He watched as the old farmhouse blew up and succumbed to fire. He noticed for the first time that Rick shot all the horses, not allowing them to burn in the fire. Compassion for animals, but not for people—a rare quality. He had plans for Rick. Tomorrow he and Omega I would issue a new strategy in their war against the rebellion of the Christians.

Promptly at ten a.m. Rick dressed in his Guardian uniform and arrived at the headquarters of the Prophet and Omega I. He'd learned through several interviews that the Prophet's name was not given to him lightly. The Prophet read minds, so Rick would have to be careful. He also radiated an aura of dark energy. Rick wondered if he ever slept.

The Prophet's secretary seemed to have defrosted a little from his last visit. At least the corners of her mouth turned up slightly now when he presented himself for a meeting.

"Go in, Mr. Hathaway. They are expecting you."

Rick entered the Prophet's office. What an unbelievable turn of events the short imprisonment had created for him—a real chance to show his stuff. And now he, Rick Hathaway, Guardian assigned to the Prophet, would meet Omega I in person. Rick took a deep breath and walked through the door. The president's back was towards him but when the Prophet greeted him, the president turned around, extending his hand.

"So you're the young man the Prophet has been telling me about—the man with the mission. The Prophet says you wish to be assigned to my personal guard duty." He exchanged glances with the Prophet. "But we think we can find a more profitable way to use your talents. You see, I watched your video."

For the first time in his life, Rick felt humble. Omega I had seen his work.

"What did you say they called the old farm?"

"Liberty Farm, sir."

"And who exactly lived there?"

"An older couple, some ranch hands..."

"That's all?"

"I think people passed through it. I'm sure Daniel Jordan and his friend did. I found their prison scrubs shoved under a bed."

"They took you in...because?"

"Because their scouts found me after I escaped Leavenworth."

The president smiled at the Prophet. "Shall we say after you *left* Leavenworth?"

"Yes, sir. It seemed to be a halfway house."

"You believe they sheltered dissidents?"

"Absolutely."

"So you..."

Rick's face reddened. "I stopped their illegal activity, Mr. President."

"Job well done. I understand Liberty Farm will never house dissidents again."

"No, sir."

"That brings us to a new challenge, Rick. Would you like to work with the Prophet on a new initiative directed toward discovering the underground Christian network and eliminating their safe houses?"

Rick couldn't believe his ears. "I'd be honored, Mr. President."

"Then you are in the hands of my good friend, the Prophet. I will be leaving for Babylon soon. Good luck, Rick." The president left the room.

"Sit down, Rick," the Prophet instructed. "Now let's think things out. No doubt, you damaged the Christian network." He hesitated, then continued, "It would have helped our cause, however, if at least one person survived. Do you understand my meaning?"

"I do, sir. Someone to interrogate, someone to unlock the secrets of the Christian underground."

The Prophet acknowledged Rick's thought process. "I want you to go undercover. Develop friendships with dissidents, begin with your friend Daniel Jordan. I assume you know his family. See what you can learn. If you discover other halfway houses, we will deal with them."

"Yes, sir."

Rick left the Prophet's office with mixed feelings: awed to have met Omega I and scared to be playing with the big boys. He reminded himself that in this job there was no room for failure.

Chapter Thirty-six

The wind bit into Lydia's cheeks. She told herself that she and Daniel were just two ordinary people taking a motorcycle ride on a lovely fall day and yet...she still felt like hiding. She drew closer to Daniel burying her head in his back as the motorcycle raced along Highway 7—a two-lane scenic highway with less risk.

As wanted criminals, they would be recognized by any security scanner. Her stomach churned and her head ached. *What if they were recognized when they stopped for fuel? What if they couldn't get to a safe house? What if...they were sent back to Leavenworth?* Lydia shook herself, trying to police the negative thoughts that bombarded her mind.

She forced herself to study the scenery. Tall maples and oaks lined the roadway touched with autumn color. Now and then rows of giant evergreens marched along the path of the motorcycle. The sun felt warm on her back and she was thankful they were free. Free...the word brought thoughts of prison—Leavenworth. She pushed memories of the brutal woman who stripped her, chopped her hair, and planted fear in her heart. Enough. That was the past. She thought of her parents, trying to survive as dissidents, and wondered how they were doing.

San Diego.

"Look out this window and tell me what you see?" Laura Cohen said to her husband.

"A man with an umbrella."

"That man has been watching our house for two days."

"Are you sure, dear?"

"Of course, I'm sure. Why don't you go out and ask him what he wants?"

Samuel Cohen wasn't sure that was a good idea. At seventy-two, he was worldly enough to suspect the man had something to do with Lydia, the child of his fifties. Or even worse, did someone suspect that he and his wife were dissidents?

The strange letter received after the unveiling of the City of Gold advised them not to try to discover Lydia's whereabouts. A threat. She had not contacted them and the last they'd seen her was spring break when she'd come home to visit. Had something happened? Why was the government watching their house now? Did the "watcher" think Lydia would return home? Perhaps Samuel would encounter the man and discover his purpose.

Samuel put on a hat, took his walking stick and a letter needing mailing, and walked down the hill to his mailbox, keeping one eye on the man who continued to stare. Samuel was a retired mathematics professor and one thing that irritated him was an unfinished equation. Where did this watcher fit into their equation?

Crossing the street he approached the man in the raincoat. "Sir, I believe you are watching our home." He paused tapping his walking stick. "Is that correct?"

The overweight, balding man nodded, his steely eyes lifeless.

Samuel changed his tactics, sensing he would get no answers on the street. "Would you care for a cup of tea or something stronger? My wife and I are curious as to why we are under surveillance."

The man shrugged his shoulders indicating he wasn't against Samuel's suggestion. They climbed the hill slowly, the watcher matching his gait to Samuel's. When they arrived at the front door, Samuel opened it, hung his hat and coat on the hall coat tree, shook out his umbrella, and leaned his walking stick against the wall; then turning, he took the man's raincoat placing it also on the coat tree.

"Follow me," Samuel said, leading him into his study. "What is your pleasure?"

"A scotch."

Samuel poured him a scotch on the rocks and turned on the gas log. "Now, we are two civilized human beings. Why don't you tell me why you are watching us."

"I am watching for your daughter, Lydia, sir."

"And you suspect she is here, or is coming here?" Samuel asked.

"It is my assignment."

"So you know that she has not contacted us?"

The man colored.

"You are monitoring our communications?"

The watcher smiled.

"Could you possibly tell me anything about our daughter? As your surveillance has shown, no doubt, you realize we know nothing. I assume you don't know where she is either and that is why you are watching our home."

The man took his time finishing his scotch. "I'm not privileged to share that information with you. I am, however, no danger to you. I made myself visible to make it easier on us both. If you receive any attempts by your daughter to contact you, you will let me know. It will go much easier on you. Do you understand?"

"Quite." Samuel stood up, anxious now to remove the unwanted guest from his home which somehow felt violated by the man's presence. He turned his back. So Lydia escaped the government's hands. But why had she left the beautiful new capital and why had she given up a job of a lifetime?

Lydia's thoughts turned to her parents. On her last visit home, her father told her they would not take the number so, like the Christians who refused the number, they were dissidents. She feared for their safety. *Did they still love her? What had they been told? Would she ever see them again?* Her scholarly parents were old and rigid. It would be hard for them to understand why she left the Youth Council. Further, the news that she'd become a Christian would upset them. She sighed.

But Lydia had no regrets…if it weren't for the exile to Leavenworth, she wouldn't know Jesus. Up to now, religion had no place in her parents' educated and controlled lives. Did they believe in God? She didn't know. Amazed at His ability to guide, protect, and help her and Daniel, a new hunger stirred in her to learn more about Christ. What had Jesus taught? She felt ashamed that she knew so little about God and had even shunned classmates who'd gone to church thinking them out of step with today. Yet, God revealed Himself to her anyway.

Daniel chose a wooded area to stop for a rest. They would have to relieve themselves in nature. "Go ahead, Lydia. I'll stay here and watch the motorcycle."

Lydia stretched and walked into the woods, trying to loosen up her muscles which had cramped from being fixed in one position. At least, nature was better than the filthy prison latrines.

She worried about the gasoline. What would they do to refill the motorcycle? She understood the Black Mustang charged its hybrid motor while they rode but sooner or later they would need gas. She looked over her shoulder at Daniel who stood by the motorcycle. He was quiet today. Something was wrong.

It felt good to wear regular clothes again. With his unlimited expense account, Rick purchased golf shirts, khakis, and even some Arizona State sweatshirts. His first stop would be Daniel's family on the guest ranch. *What was his little sister's name?*

Rick parked his SUV in front of the ranch, wondering who would be home on a Saturday. Daniel's sister opened the door. A look of recognition crossed her face.

"Hi, you're Rick, aren't you? Come in. I'll call my mom."

"No, that's all right. Penny, isn't it."

Penny blushed. This was Daniel's old partner. He was handsome. "Okay."

"I'm trying to track Daniel down. I sort of lost track of him when they sent him to Fort Thompson."

Penny wasn't sure she should be talking to Rick without her parents.

"I'm not a Guardian anymore. Wanted to see what Daniel was up to." Rick waited on Penny's response. Just then Daniel's mother came out of her office.

Surprised to see Rick, she wondered if he was still picking up dissidents. She hoped Harry didn't come in for supper while Rick was here. "Rick, how are you. Saw you on the news picking up dissidents under the bridge."

Well that was too bad, Rick thought. "Yeah, I'm not a Guardian anymore, Mrs. Jordan. Just wondered what happened to Daniel after he left the Fort. I'm at ASU now working on a business degree." The lie came easily.

Anger clouded Mrs. Jordan's face. "You've come to the wrong place, Rick. We have no son. Just Penny."

Puzzled, Rick didn't understand. He looked at Penny who'd gasped when her mother answered, tears blurring her eyes.

"Mother, how can you say that? He's still our Daniel even if we don't know where he is."

"I think you should go, Rick. Daniel is a sore spot in our family. He gave up his job at the Youth Council in the City of Gold and no one appears to know where he is. He is out of our life."

"I'm sorry, Mrs. Jordan. What happened to Daniel's motorcycle? I might want to buy it."

Judith recovered. "Harry gave it to one of Daniel's high school friends, Joey. He's a student in veterinary medicine at University of Arizona. Doubt he'd want to sell it."

What did Penny's frown mean?

"Walk me out, Pen?"

Penny walked Rick to the door. "Something wrong, Penny?"

Upset with her mother, Penny replied. "Joey doesn't have the motorcycle."

Rick left. He'd learned one piece of valuable information. Maybe Daniel had his motorcycle and was using it to escape. *But how would he have gotten it?*

Rick wondered if Mr. Jordan held the key to the whereabouts of the motorcycle. He decided not to try to interview Daniel's dad. Wanting to waste no more time, Rick decided to go with the clue about the motorcycle. Perhaps if he returned to Liberty Farm and looked for the most direct roads to the border, he'd discover Daniel's trail.

Daniel bent over several times, throwing his arms over his head to break the tightness in his shoulders and back. When Lydia returned, he gave her a hug and walked into the woods. Back on the highway, he headed north taking small two-lane highways. Lydia was amazed that he never got lost, yet changed highways to stay on the less traveled.

Shadows under the trees grew darker and the moon came out. While at Liberty Farm, Bill suggested they try to reach the Kilen State Park which was just over the Minnesota state line. The park ended its season on Labor Day weekend. Bill wasn't sure whether day charges were made to enter the park, but if Daniel and Lydia entered after dark and left before nine a.m. they should be all right. Whether there was water for showers was questionable as the park turned off the water before winter.

Tired from long hours of riding on the motorcycle, Lydia was relieved when Daniel pulled into the park. They drove past campsites for recreational vehicles looking for the sites tent campers used. Finally, about a half mile into the park, they spotted some sites. Daniel parked and helped Lydia off the cycle.

"Let's gather some wood. I don't know if there are any wild animals but they are usually afraid of a fire."

Within a few minutes they had gathered enough branches for a nice fire. Daniel spread out their sleeping bags while Lydia got out the jerky and some hard rolls and cheese provided by Martha before they left.

"Daniel, you're so quiet. Do you want to tell me what you're thinking about?"

"I feel bad that I've put you in so much danger."

"I know, Daniel. But I made my own decision. You're my friend. I couldn't stand to see them mistreating you. We hadn't committed any crime. I never thought they'd put us in prison."

"But they did."

"Yes, but something wonderful happened even in prison. I met Jesus. My parents are respectable people but they don't know God. I didn't know He was alive or that He cared for us. Look what He did! He got us out of Leavenworth. He brought the pastor and your father together and inspired your father to drive your motorcycle to Liberty Farm. He gave us Bill and Martha to take care of us and hide us. I just can't imagine what He'll do next. Can't you see His fingerprints in our lives?" A giant smile lit Lydia's face and for a moment all pain was forgotten.

Daniel took her hands. Lydia's words soothed his heart. He stroked her hair and then kissed her.

"Have you been planning that all day, Danny?"

"Of course."

"How long will it take us to get across the border?"

"A day or so…I guess."

"And gas? Do we dare use the gas card?"

"We're too close to the prison. I don't think we can take any chances."

Lydia curled up next to Daniel. She closed her eyes and prayed, *"Dear God, you are the only reason we are free. Thank you. Guide us; protect us. You are all we have."*

Light rainfall awoke the young couple. Despite the hard ground, they'd slept soundly. The aroma of bacon, eggs, and coffee reached them from a neighboring camper. Then a voice called, "You young people like a hot cup of java?"

Someone had been watching them. "Thank you, sir. A hot drink would really warm us up."

"Sleeping under the stars gets a little cold sometimes, even when you're young."

"Yes, it does." Daniel and Lydia cradled the cups of coffee in their hands, warming their hands before sipping the steaming brew. Alert to the danger, Daniel didn't wish to carry on a conversation with the strangers.

"Me and the wife like to sneak in here each fall—her favorite time of year. Cheaper, too. Too bad they turn the water off; it'd be nice to get a shower. At least the vaults are working."

"Vaults?"

"Yeah, the port-a-potties we used to call them. Beats the bushes. Name's Frank, wife's Carol. Where you young people headed?" the man asked.

A red light went on in Daniel's heart. He signaled Lydia with his eyes. "Haven't decided yet. But thanks for the coffee. Sir, you wouldn't happen to have a little extra gas, would you? I can't pay you. We don't have any money."

"Yeah, I guess so. I carry an extra five-gallon can with me. What's it take, about three?"

"Three would be great." Daniel beamed.

"That's all right, boy. We need to look out for each other in this world, don't cha think?"

Daniel took the can from Frank and filled up the motorcycle. "Thanks, we appreciate it."

"Don't mention it. I can fill my can up when I go into town. Have a safe one."

Daniel and Lydia mounted the motorcycle anxious to leave the couple before they asked too many questions.

"Do you think they're suspicious, Daniel? Will they notify the police?"

"I'm hoping they think we eloped and are running away. But if they do report us, they'll have to answer questions about why they were in the park when it was closed so..."

Carol turned to Frank. "Of course, we know they are runaways. Do you think it's possible there's a reward?"

"Don't know. After we pack up, we can alert the police. Depends on whether they're dissidents. I'll describe the young couple. Sorry, I didn't snap a picture with my communicator. Maybe the police can tell us if their parents offer a reward. Worth a try. A reward will more than cover the three gallons I gave them. They headed straight down Highway 7."

Chapter Thirty-seven

Rick wished he'd left one of the people alive at the Farm. He poked the ashes and rubble with his walking stick surprised to see no bones from the explosion and fire.

"What are you doing, boy?"

Two men dressed roughly in farm clothes appeared from behind the bushes.

Startled Rick remembered to be undercover. "Something terrible happen here?"

"You could say that. Looks like the farm got burned down. Too bad, nice people Bill and Martha. Weren't you the boy that they helped who escaped from Leavenworth?"

"Yeah, wanted to come back and thank them. Were they killed?"

"No." Wary, remembering Rick's Guardian uniform, they clammed up.

"I'd think anyone in the house would have been killed with this kind of fire. Looks like an explosion blew the windows out." Rick walked around, surprised the horses he'd shot were missing. "Did you guys used to work on the ranch?"

The two hands looked at each other, thinking it might be a good time to lie. "No, just neighbors. Sad to lose nice people. We buried the horses."

Used to tracking from his Guardian training, Rick noticed two sets of tire prints in the dirt—one tire marks from a motorcycle and one probably from an RV. He started the motorcycle he'd purchased in order to get an idea of how far Daniel and the girl could go in a day.

"Sorry about the fire," Rick said. "Guess I'll be going." He grinned. Detective work was a lot more interesting than guard duty at Leavenworth. Now he could follow the RV tracks or stay on course to find Daniel and the girl. Since Daniel and the girl were a higher priority, he followed the tracks of the motorcycle.

Lydia leaned into Daniel's body letting him shield her from the drizzle. If they could find gas one more time, they'd make it to the border. At five o'clock, when the fuel gauge was hovering near empty, Daniel rolled into the small town of Blackduck Lake, Minnesota—residents 785, at least that's what it said on the sign. Just outside the town they discovered the lake. As they reached the shoreline, a cloud of black mallards rose into the sky frightened by the motorcycle's roar. The cold drizzle had chased away any fishermen and the summer cottages appeared to be closed up for the winter.

"We've got to get out of the rain," said Daniel. He parked the cycle next to an old shed belonging to one of the small log cabins. Turning, he lifted Lydia gently down beside him, noticing the raindrops running down her face. Unable to resist, he bent over and kissed her lightly on the cheek then hurried her to the shed. He tried the door but found it locked from the inside.

"This window isn't quite shut," called Lydia. Daniel watched her as she tried to open it, but it wouldn't budge.

"Wait honey, don't break it." Daniel moved to the window and Lydia backed away to let him have a try. He pressed on the pane, but the window still wouldn't budge. He looked for something to pry it open, spotting a branch lying in a puddle. He shoved the tip of the branch under the ledge like a lever and pushed. Finally, the window, which probably hadn't been opened in years, raised an inch. Daniel shoved with all his strength and it broke loose.

"Do you think you can squeeze through the opening if I boost you up?" He cupped his hands and Lydia stepped into them, lunging for the half-open window. Cobwebs and dirt tangled her hair but she paid no attention. She dropped down, trying to avoid an old lawnmower and letting her eyes get used to the dim light.

"There's a door. I'll try to unbolt it." She slid the bar releasing the bolt. The ancient door groaned as it opened to let in a soaked Daniel.

Happy to be out of the rain, the two explored the inside of the shed. Daniel lifted an empty flowerpot and discovered a box of matches.

"I found a couple of lawn chairs with cushions," said Lydia. "Maybe we could sleep in here tonight."

At the house next door, Mack and Anna Adams watched the young people climb in the window of the neighbor's shed.

"Call the sheriff, Mack. They're breaking in."

"Let's watch. They're soaked to the skin riding that motorcycle. Maybe they just need a dry place to wait out the storm."

"They're vagrants. I don't like it. At least call the Miles. Tell them someone is breaking into their shed. Ask them what they want us to do."

"Relax, Anna. What are they going to steal? They're on a motorcycle. We'll keep an eye out. We can always call Sheriff Barnes."

Continuing his search through the dusty shed, Daniel spotted a cane fishing pole leaning against the far wall. "When the rain lets up, I'll see what I can catch for supper."

"You know how to fish?" Lydia looked at Daniel doubtfully. "You grew up in the desert."

"I used to fish with my grandfather every summer in Michigan. He lived on a lake just like this one." Daniel wished he had one of Grandpa's nice lures for bait but maybe with the rain, he'd find a nightcrawler.

Nose pressed to the dirty window, Lydia looked out towards the water, "I think the rain stopped, but it's really foggy."

Daniel finished tying a hook onto the line. "Let's go fishing," he said pushing the door open for Lydia.

Outside, they circled the shed and Daniel spotted an old log. Rolling it over, he scratched the dirt, finally holding up a fat night crawler. Tying a knot in the worm Daniel wove the hook through the worm. Looking up he caught a startled look on Lydia's face.

"It's okay, city girl, they don't feel anything and we need to eat. I think this lake will have some big fish."

Walking through the wet grass, Lydia followed Daniel to the shore line. She longed for ordinary food: a hamburger, French fries, fried chicken, or a steak. But these weren't ordinary times. She would be thankful for whatever supper they could find—even fish.

Daniel cast his line into the tall weeds growing next to the sea wall.

"Why are you casting here?" Lydia asked.

"They like to hide in the tall weeds, especially in the fall."

Lydia watched Daniel as he patiently cast and recast the line.

Suddenly he felt a sharp tug on the line, "Whoa!" he yelled, trying to regain his balance. "Nearly pulled me in."

He wrestled with the fish for a few moments, finally pulling out the ugliest two-foot-long creature Lydia had ever seen. She backed away, "What kind of fish is it? It's so ugly; look at its teeth!"

"It's a walleye. Don't let his looks scare you, he's great eating."

"How 'bout I start a fire? I think I saw some logs covered with a tarp that might be drier. Toss me the matches and I'll get started while you fish."

"Get away from that window, Anna," Mack said.

"He caught a big walleye with the neighbor's pole. She's starting a fire. Wonder what else they're gonna steal?"

Mack shook his head. "So they stole a night crawler and a few logs."

"They're probably homeless dissidents. I don't like it, Mack. They got no right to break into that shed. If you don't call Sheriff Barnes, I'll call him."

"Let's wait and see if they're still here in the morning," Mack said.

"Well, did you like the walleye?"

"You are a gourmet cook, monsieur."

It was dark now but the fire took the chill off and soon their clothes, soaked while they were riding the motorcycle, were drying. In the glow of the firelight, Daniel moved closer to Lydia. Putting his arm around her, he drew her close.

"Some romance, huh?" he grinned.

"Right out of the storybooks."

"And which story would that be, my lady, 'Beauty and the Beast'?"

"Daniel, be serious."

"Would you like to read a little before we go to bed?"

"I'd love it."

Walking over to his motorcycle, Daniel took out the wooden box with the Bible. Bringing it over to Lydia, he sat down and opened the old book to a favorite part he'd discovered in the gospel of John. "Elizabeth probably told you that Jesus chose twelve men to follow him—the disciples. One of these was John who wrote down many of Jesus' teachings and miracles. I love the way he begins. Listen to this, Lydia."

In the beginning was the word,

And the Word was with God.

He was in the beginning with God

All things came into being through Him,

And without Him nothing came into being.

In him was life, and the life was the light of all people

The light shines in the darkness.

And the darkness did not overcome it (NASB)

"It's so beautiful, like poetry. Do you think the Word means Jesus?"

"I hadn't thought about that," Daniel replied. "If it does, then Jesus helped with the creation of the world."

"And ...it says He is the light. He was our light—a light in our prison." Lydia grew very quiet. "Daniel, we should read the stories of Jesus every day until we know Him." She took the Bible out of his hands and something fell out.

"What's this?" Lydia picked up the folded piece of paper.

"It's a map showing some safe houses for the Christian underground."

"All of them?"

"Not all of them, I think it's just a pencil sketch sent to my grandfather by his Michigan pastor. See there's Liberty Farm right outside of Leavenworth." Daniel noticed an area circled in Canada." I think we might be close to the one in Canada. It looks like it's on the other side of a river. We can't be too far from there."

Lydia held the white stone closer to the fire so she could see it. "Do you know what this stone is for?"

"No, looks like someone carved a dove on it." He shoved it into his jacket pocket. They put out the campfire and returned to the shed. A few stars peeked through the clouds, providing enough light to find their way.

Lydia climbed into a lawn chair and Daniel spread his jacket over her to keep her warm. He brushed the soft brown hair off her cheek, overcome by a rush of feelings. Taking an old flannel shirt smelling of fish off a nail in the shed, he moved his lawn chair next to hers and covered himself up. *Lord, thank you for Lydia.*

The next morning the motorcycle was still there. "I'm calling the sheriff. It's not right. They're thieves," said Anna.

Mack decided not to cross his wife. "Let me do it, Anna."

"Sheriff Barnes here. Is this an emergency?"

"Well my wife thinks so. Mack Adams, sheriff. Two young people broke into the Miles' shed. We kinda take care of it when they leave in the fall."

"Where are they now?"

"Think they're still in the shed. Went in through the window last night."

"Can you describe them?"

"It was kinda dark. Young enough to crawl in a window, jeans, jackets. Couldn't really tell if it was two boys or a boy and a girl till we saw them cuddled up by the fire. Rode in on a black Honda motorcycle."

"Well," said the sheriff, "what did they steal?"

"So far as I can see just some night crawlers, a few logs, and a couple of walleyes. But it's the principle of the thing. They shouldn't be going into someone else's property through a window. Just thought you should know. A lot of thieving going around these lakes."

The sheriff sighed and said, "Tell you what, I'll come out and take a look."

Sheriff Barnes parked his old Ford Crown Victoria on the stone parking area behind the shed where it was less muddy. Getting out of the car, he walked around to the front of the shed. Daniel, who'd been searching for gas, heard a tap on the windowpane. Startled, he looked up to see the sheriff in the window.

"What's going on, son? Stealing a little gasoline for your motorcycle?" The sheriff pushed his way into the shed. "Neighbors tell me you broke in last night."

Tongue-tied, Daniel didn't answer. In truth, he'd just found a five-gallon can of gas under a pile of life jackets and his plan was to use the gas to fill his motorcycle. Caught in the act, he had no answer for the sheriff.

"Where's your friend? They reported two of you."

Daniel's eyes wandered over to the corner. The sheriff followed his gaze noting Lydia standing by an old freezer.

"And what might you be doing, Miss? Stealing fish from their freezer?"

Lydia shook her head. "No, sir, I'm putting these fish Daniel caught into the freezer as a thank you for giving us shelter from the rain."

The sheriff put a call in on his communicator. "Sam, got a home invasion over here at Black Duck Lake. I'll need you to send a trailer and bring their motorcycle to the station. Right, the Miles' cottage."

He turned. "Unfortunately, kids, I'm taking you in."

Daniel and Lydia climbed into the backseat and sat down in silence. Lydia's face lost all its color. She'd never been in a police car before.

"It's over, Danny."

Daniel signaled her not to talk.

"Better think of some good reasons for me not to put you in jail. One thing we don't like around here are thieves." The sheriff started the motor and edged the car onto the road.

What could they say to the sheriff? Their fate was in his hands. Daniel put his arm around Lydia, feeling her tremble. "I don't think God set us free with a miracle only to have us be caught," he whispered. "Let's pray that He'll help us."

Chapter Thirty-eight

Sheriff Barnes turned off the engine of the old car as they parked in front of a small, weather-beaten building labeled Sheriff's Office. "Time to get out, folks."

"What will you do with my motorcycle, sir?"

The sheriff looked thoughtful. "The question really is, son, what will I do with you?"

He led them into his office and told them to sit down. He checked his computer to see if these two were runaways and...if there was a reward. A bulletin caught the sheriff's eye. "Keep on the lookout for two Leavenworth escapees probably headed for the border on a black motorcycle." The sheriff looked up, aware the two young people sitting in front of him were probably the two escapees. He cleared his throat. "Now, why don't you fill me in on your story...no fiction, got it."

Daniel swallowed, exchanging anxious looks with Lydia.

Tell him your story, Daniel.

I can't, Lord, he'll send me back to prison.

Trust me.

"Sir, my friend and I escaped from Leavenworth prison."

Lydia inhaled sharply, *Why was Daniel telling the sheriff who they really were?* She stared wide-eyed at Daniel, but bit her lip.

"Good grief, boy, why were you in Leavenworth? What did you do?"

"We were exiled by the Prophet from the City of Gold while we were on the Youth Council," Daniel explained. "I refused to bow to a golden statue. Lydia saw the Prophet's men throw me to the ground and left the line to make sure I was all right. The Prophet's guards turned us over to the Prophet and the next thing we knew, they put us in prison."

"The prison was full of homeless people and dissidents," Lydia picked up the story. "They starved us. Daniel had to dig graves for the people donating their organs. They said everyone in Leavenworth was in prison for life. I didn't think we'd ever get out."

Daniel continued, "We escaped with God's help, but we are wanted and if you turn us over to the authorities, we will probably be executed."

"God, huh?" The sheriff rubbed his forehead. "The Prophet is no favorite of mine. Government's gone to hell in a handbasket."

The sheriff couldn't help noting fear and sadness in the young lady's eyes. He got up and walked outside, leaving Daniel and Lydia to wonder what he planned to do with them. They watched through the window as the deputy rolled Daniel's motorcycle down a trailer ramp.

When Sheriff Barnes returned, he looked Daniel and Lydia up and down—two teenagers, homeless and on the run, unable to go home, looking half-starved. "Let me see if I have your story straight. You needed shelter from the rain, is that right? Then you stole a couple of worms, caught a couple of walleyes, made a campfire, and slept in the shed. Have I got it right?"

Daniel and Lydia nodded.

"Were you planning to steal gas?"

Daniel dropped his head. "It was the only way we could make it to the border."

"Do you have anything you could pay these people for, say, if you'd stolen gas?"

Lydia spoke up. "We've been afraid to use our gas card. We could trade it for the gas."

"I'll let you go, providing you turn that gas card over to me. That should satisfy the Adams."

Daniel searched in his jacket pocket for the gas card. "Thank you, sir. Thank you so much."

"Anything I can do to annoy the government. Done nothing but make life harder. None of our old folks allowed in the hospitals, forcing everyone to get a number. Makes so many homeless, I need to build a motel to put them in. Then, you got your folks like the Adams...well, you get the picture."

"Where you folks headed?"

Daniel and Lydia traded a glance with each other, but remained silent.

"If you're planning to go through a border checkpoint, I wouldn't if I were you. Your faces on some kinda wanted list for messing with the Prophet?"

"Yes, sir."

"They've got Guardians just waiting for dissidents. Heard they shot one trying to cross the other day. Real dangerous. Find another way."

Afraid to ask, Daniel said, "You got any suggestions for us, sheriff?

"Wish I could help. There aren't any fences but they got searchlights along the border. Laser beams all along either side of the border checkpoints. Break that beam and it triggers the checkpoint and sends a task force out to find you.

"Only one place within a hundred miles you got a chance crossing the border…at Rainey River. I hunt and fish up there sometimes." The sheriff paused. "There's a border crossing at Baudette. Take Highway 72 north. Just before you get to Baudette, turn and go east for about eleven miles along the river. You'll be at Clementson. There's an old resort. Might have a chance to cross the Rainey there. But remember, the river's patrolled too."

"How far is it?" Daniel asked.

"A hundred, hundred and fifty miles. Since I got your gas card, I'll fill your tanks for you. You'll have enough gas to get there. Don't know how you'll get across."

Daniel shook hands with the sheriff. "Thanks again, sir."

"No problem."

Lydia surprised the sheriff by reaching up to give him a hug.

Time was of the essence for Rick. He'd sent out a bulletin calling attention to the fact that Daniel and Lydia escaped Leavenworth and were likely riding a black Honda motorcycle. Afraid the two were near the border, he pulled into a sleepy little town called Black Duck Lake searching for the sheriff's office. Since five border crossings appeared on the GPS, Rick needed information from the sheriff on which might be the least patrolled.

Rick parked the motorcycle outside the sheriff's office and walked into the office.

"Sheriff Barnes. Can I help you?"

Rick took out his credentials and flashed them in front of the sheriff. "I need some information on the border crossings, sheriff. Can you tell me which border crossings would be easiest for dissidents to cross?"

Sheriff Barnes scratched his head. "Well, dissidents don't have much luck at these border crossings. Lots of Guardians, laser beams and floodlights. Were you looking for some particular dissidents? Maybe I can keep my eyes open for you."

Rick pulled out pictures of Daniel and Lydia. "These people escaped Leavenworth and I've been sent to track them."

"How was that possible?" asked the sheriff. "I thought the dissident prison was impenetrable."

"We don't know. The Prophet has a high reward out for their capture. He thinks it may have been an inside job. Doesn't want other attempts."

The sheriff scrutinized Rick keeping his personal reaction hidden."

"Can't help you, but I can tell you that the western border crossing might be the easiest to break through. These other four have pretty good laser technology and tight controls. Good luck to you. I'll keep watch on this end."

Rick left the office and headed west. The question was, had Daniel and Lydia already made it across the border? Was he too late?

The young couple climbed on the cycle following the sheriff's general directions. After riding a couple of hours, they turned east on Highway 11 which was definitely a scenic highway along the Rainey River. Highly forested with tall, ancient pine trees, the road ran along the river which didn't appear wide but according to the sheriff was eighty miles long. A tattered sign, barely legible, announced the town of Clementson, Minnesota.

Soon the resort came into view situated atop a rolling hill. Eight small weather-beaten cabins probably built in the early 1900s, plus a small business building, reflected the unkempt appearance of the lawn. Lydia and Daniel stopped, parked the motorcycle at the base of the hill, and hiked up the tall grassy incline to get a better view. The setting sun turned the sky shades of orange and purple. Ahead of them they saw a wooden pier where a small rowboat with a motor and a large, light blue houseboat were fastened.

"You looking to go to Canada?"

Daniel and Lydia turned to see a tall, dark-haired boy covered in tattoos and wearing a long dangling earring. They didn't reply.

"Runaways come through here all the time. If you're willing to deal, you can leave the Honda and take the fishing boat."

"And when we get on board, you'll report us to the authorities, right?"

The kid smiled. "I guess that's the risk you take."

Daniel's gut told him the kid was a trickster. He pulled Lydia aside. "Do you trust him?"

"No, Danny, he looks like a drug addict. I don't think we can trust him."

Frustrated, Daniel whispered, "He'll report us either way. Maybe it's worth a chance. He wants the motorcycle."

"But your dad gave it to you to use to have a safe way to…"

"It served its purpose. We can't get across water on it." Daniel reached in the saddlebags removing the small carved box with the Bible. "Hide this under your jacket, Lydia. Don't let him see it. Let's go."

They hiked back up the hill reaching the kid as he tried to start the old motor on the fishing boat. It sputtered and coughed, then broke into a small roar.

Daniel tossed the motorcycle key to the boy who caught it in his fist.

"C'mon, Lydia. Don't slip." He steadied the boat while Lydia climbed in and sat down her feet in a couple inches of water from the heavy rainfall the day before. Daniel steered the boat across the river. A bright harvest moon cast a golden path across the dark water.

"I wish this were just an adventure." Lydia sighed.

"It's an adventure all right," said Daniel, pulling his eyes away from the moonlight shining on Lydia's hair to scan the river. "Keep your eyes open for a patrol boat. I'm sure they keep tight watch over this river."

"How do you know where to head?" Lydia asked.

"I don't really. I'm guessing it may be just a little west of where we're crossing, maybe in that forested area."

"Do you think that tattooed kid will be satisfied with the Honda and leave us alone?"

"I hope so."

Lydia watched the light beams search the shore. "I wonder how many make it to the checkpoint and are captured?" she asked.

"Too many, I'm afraid," said Daniel.

"Will they have laser beams along the Canadian shore, too, Danny?"

Sensing Lydia's worry, Daniel hesitated… "I don't think so."

Halfway across the river, the motor died and the boat began to drift with the current.

"Danny, we're drifting toward the checkpoint at Baudette. I can see the lights searching the river."

Daniel struggled with the old rusty motor trying to start it again. After a few pulls on the motor he realized it was flooded.

"Hand me the oars, Lydia, I'll try to row across." He secured the oars and began to row, pulling the boat in a northern direction against the current.

Lydia was shivering. "Can you pull your feet up out of the water?" Daniel asked. "That might help." He continued to row, scanning the water for the River Patrol.

Out of nowhere, a flashing light and a blast from a fog-horn startled them. Two brown-uniformed deputies grabbed hold of the rowboat pulling it next to their craft. "You folks going somewhere?" asked the deputy.

Tired of the many obstacles they'd encountered trying to get to safety, the two just nodded.

"Can I see your passports please."

Daniel and Lydia pulled the false passports Bill and Martha had given them out of their shoes and handed them over to the officers, not even looking at each other for encouragement.

There was nowhere to go this time. No escape.

"Where were you headed?" the first deputy asked studying their passports.

"Canada, sir." Daniel answered.

"How long did you plan to stay?"

"We were actually hoping to make our home there," Lydia said.

"Do you have family or friends in Canada? How do you plan to support yourselves?"

Lydia and Daniel had no answer. All hope gone.

The officer looked at Daniel and Lydia for a long time, then handed back their passports.

"Sure you're not the two young people who escaped Leavenworth? Lydia? Daniel?"

Daniel gave up. "Yes sir, that's us."

A smile broke out on the deputy's face. "Good, we've been watching for you kids…almost gave up hope. Wanted to intercept you before the American River Patrol got to you."

This was a Canadian River Patrol?

"Any chance you're hoping to join up with our village? Climb aboard. You'll be safer with us. The village is just ahead."

"The camp for dissidents?"

"That's right, we try to catch as many as we can. Got a message from Sheriff Barnes that you might be headed this way." He winked at Lydia. "He especially liked that hug you gave him."

The speedboat drifted up to a landing and Daniel lifted Lydia out of the boat and onto shore. They shook hands with the deputies who pointed them to a path going deep into the forest.

As the young couple started to walk, Lydia stopped and said, "There are no coincidences, Daniel. It's all God orchestrating this."

Slowly, the two continued through the dark pine trees carrying nothing but the little carved box Lydia had hidden under her jacket. They were in a heavily forested area. Evergreen trees lined the path. Daniel took hold of Lydia's hand. An owl hooted and a squirrel scurried across the fallen leaves as they went deeper into the forest. The moon shone brightly on the path. The temperature had dropped and the air felt crisp like it was getting ready to snow.

Unable to believe they were safe, Lydia's heart hammered, still expecting someone to stop them at any moment. About a mile down the path, lights shone over the trees. A gate barred the way. Daniel stopped in front of the gate, gathering Lydia into his arms. "I think it's really over, Lydia." He kissed her tenderly, not the kiss of a friend, but a kiss with promise.

As they stood there together, the gate swung open. Before them, they could see small log cabins tucked into the forest dotting the hill. A large log building stood in front of them with a lighted flagpole flying the Canadian flag.

"Danny, do you see it?"

A second flag snapped in the breeze beside it, a blue flag with a white dove on it.

"It's a dove, just like our stone."

Book III — 2025

"R"

The Remnant

(coming in 2013)

S.D. Burke

Sylvia Burke graduated from Indiana University with a B.S. degree in Nursing. She's worked in Public Health Nursing, Obstetrics, Emergency Room and Hospice. But... the majority of years, she was a stay-at-home wife and mother.

She published *Putting Humpty Dumpty Together Again— Christian Help for Depression* in 2002 to help people recover from grief, and depression. *2025 The Guardian* and *City of Gold* are her first fiction novels.

In retirement, Sylvia follows her passion as a Bible study teacher and facilitator often writing her own studies and curriculum.

In 2011 she and her husband George celebrated their 50th wedding anniversary. The Burkes have six children and ten grandchildren. They split their time between Michigan and Arizona and have enjoyed exploring the southwest in retirement.

Singing in a church choir, reading, quilting, watercolor painting, and gardening, are a few of her hobbies. Says Burke, "Retirement is a time to tap the rainbow in my heart and I consider every day I walk with the Lord an adventure." You are invited to join her blog at 2025sdburke.com.